HAND
OF FATE

HAND
OF FATE

Michael Underwood

PERENNIAL LIBRARY

Harper & Row, Publishers, New York
Cambridge, Philadelphia, San Francisco
London, Mexico City, São Paulo, Singapore, Sydney

HAND OF FATE. Copyright © 1981 by Michael Underwood. All rights reserved. Printed in the United States of America. No part of this book may be used or reproduced in any manner whatsoever without written permission except in the case of brief quotations embodied in critical articles and reviews. For information address St. Martin's Press, Inc., 175 Fifth Avenue, New York, New York 10010. Published simultaneously in Canada by Fitzhenry & Whiteside Limited, Toronto.

First PERENNIAL LIBRARY edition published 1987.

Library of Congress Cataloging-in-Publication Data

Underwood, Michael, 1916–
  Hand of fate.

  I. Title.
PR6055.V3H3   1987   823'.914   86-46106
ISBN 0-06-080868-3 (pbk.)

87 88 89 90 91 OMP 10 9 8 7 6 5 4 3 2 1

For Alan

Part 1

1

It is not easy to commit the perfect murder, though Frank Wimble never doubted his ability to do so. After all, as he never tired of reminding everyone, you don't start up a business on three hundred pounds and sell it twenty-five years later for three million without being possessed of the ingredients of success in life. These, he would go on to say, were ambition, hard work and complete self-confidence, plus a bit of luck and an occasional touch of ruthlessness.

He always made the element of ruthlessness sound like a tasty dash of seasoning, whereas most of his friends saw it as a great raw hunk of his character.

After twenty-seven years of marriage, nobody knew him better than his wife, Elspeth. She had borne him two children and had always seemed willing to make most of the adjustments necessitated by living with an aggressive egotist. She had even been prepared to turn a blind eye on his infidelities (those she knew about) and gone on loving him after many

3

another woman would have divorced him three times over.

And in his own faithless way he had gone on loving her until the fateful day he had met Maureen Yates. Not that there had seemed anything especially fateful about it at the time. She was eighteen years younger than he and recently divorced and they had found themselves in the same party at the Ascot July meeting. Elspeth had not been there, though her absence can hardly be said to have affected subsequent events, which from then on assumed the inevitability of one season following another.

About three months later he asked Elspeth for a divorce, a request she flatly turned down. Subsequently he was to plead, cajole and even demand, all to no avail.

In the end (this was about a year after he had set Maureen up in a flat in London) he reached the conclusion that there was only one way of resolving the situation. Elspeth would have to disappear. In those first days he thought of it as her disappearance rather than as her murder.

What drove him to this conclusion was Maureen's threat to end their relationship unless she could have him one hundred percent. *He* would have been prepared to continue with the existing arrangement, namely a mistress in London and a wife in the country, but Maureen was not, and the prospect of losing her made him realise there was only one alternative.

So it came about toward the end of September when the leaves had already begun to fall that Elspeth suddenly vanished.

One day she was there, the next she had disappeared without a trace.

Almost a week passed before anyone remarked upon her absence (for the Wimbles were frequently away from home) and then it was no more than a casual enquiry by Mrs. Drake who, with her husband, ran the village general store.

"Mrs. Wimble all right, is she?" she said to Mrs. Passingham who was the Wimbles' daily help.

"She's away," Mrs. Passingham replied in what seemed to be an unnecessarily tight-lipped manner. But then, to the chagrin of her neighbours, Ada Passingham had never been one to indulge in gossip, which most of them regarded as a terrible waste of opportunity on the part of someone who worked in a number of Little Misten's well-heeled homes.

"She was called suddenly to the sickbed of her aunt," Mrs. Passingham now added unexpectedly.

"Where does her aunt live?" Mrs. Drake enquired, encouraged by this gratuitously given piece of information.

Mrs. Passingham shook her head, however. "Don't know."

"Expecting her to be away long, are you?" Mrs. Drake said with still flickering hope.

"He didn't say how long."

"*He?*" Mrs. Drake sounded puzzled.

"Mr. Wimble. It was he what told me when I got there last Saturday. Said his wife had been called away sudden the previous night."

"I'm sorry to hear that," Mrs. Drake said. "Nice woman she is. Always gets on well with everyone in the village. Can't say the same for him."

She threw the other woman a covert glance, but Mrs. Passingham was not to be drawn further and merely stood waiting in a forbidding silence for the quarter pound of English cheddar she had gone in to buy.

And there the matter rested for several weeks. After all, everyone knew that sick aunts could linger

5

on and it wasn't as if there was anything to bring her home in a hurry apart from Mr. Wimble and he, as everyone also knew, was here, there and everywhere making more money all the time. He might have sold his business, but he certainly hadn't retired.

During the course of these weeks, he was seen only on intermittent occasions in the village, usually driving through in his tan-coloured Mercedes on his way to or from Downview Lodge, the Wimbles' home a mile and a half outside Little Misten.

It was a sunny Saturday morning about six weeks after his wife's disappearance that he was spotted driving along the main street with an attractive young woman in the seat beside him. The next morning when he came into the village to buy Sunday papers, he also purchased a copy of a women's weekly magazine which he said he had been specially asked to get.

These seemingly innocent events were soon fused together in a train of gossip which eventually reached the ears of young Police Constable Jameson who was Little Misten's chief guardian of law and order.

He was attached to the police station of a neighbouring, and larger, village and was accustomed to visit Little Misten in his panda car two or three times a week or whenever there was a special call for his presence.

He was a keen young officer who kept an alert ear to the ground and so it didn't take long for the wilder rumours about what had happened to Elspeth Wimble to reach him.

Being a judicious young man, and though aware of plentiful examples in history of husbands murdering their wives and disposing secretly of their bodies, he decided he should check and cross-check the rumours as well as he could before making any report to his superiors.

In the event, however, he soon ran into a dead end. All that he was able to establish was that Mrs. Wimble had abruptly disappeared from her home nearly two months earlier and had not been seen around since. It also seemed to be proven that her husband had entertained another woman at Downview Lodge during a recent weekend.

Even a dumb country copper can see that doesn't add up to murder, he reflected wistfully. On the other hand, a few discreet enquiries seemed called for.

"There's never smoke without a fire," Mrs. Drake had said darkly after taking him into the room behind the shop and firmly closing the door so that they wouldn't be disturbed. "What's more," she went on, "he's just the sort of man who would murder his wife."

"What makes you say that?" Bob Jameson asked cautiously.

"You only have to talk to him for half a minute to know. Ready to squash anyone who gets in his way."

"I've always found him all right."

"Well, you would, wouldn't you! He'd go out of his way not to upset you, seeing you're a policeman."

Bob Jameson said nothing, but remembered the countless motorists who hadn't shrunk from abusing him when reproved for some minor traffic offence.

"He was really nasty to Fred on one occasion because we didn't have any of his fancy cigarettes in stock."

"I'm sure Mr. Drake was able to look after himself," Jameson said with a faint smile.

After leaving Drake's Stores, he sat thinking in his car for a while. Even if Mr. Wimble were to be at home, which was unlikely, an approach at this juncture would undoubtedly be premature. After all, he could scarcely accost him and say, "I'd be grateful if you would confirm or deny the rumours that you've done away with your wife."

If and when that moment should arrive, it would obviously be a job for the C.I.D. and Jameson wouldn't be thanked if he had queered their pitch in advance.

He glanced at his watch and saw that it was ten minutes before one. It might be a good moment to call on Mrs. Passingham. She would be at home preparing the midday meal before setting out again to one of her afternoon jobs. She mightn't be very pleased to see him, but that was a risk he was prepared to take.

The Passinghams lived in an isolated cottage about half a mile from the village. Mr. Passingham had worked on a nearby farm until succumbing to a stroke, since when he had become entirely dependent on his wife. He had never fully recovered his speech and he could walk only with the help of two sticks. Most of his day was spent sitting in a chair with a newspaper resting on his lap.

A smell of fried onions greeted P.C. Jameson as he approached the side door of the cottage. Through the window he could see Mrs. Passingham at the stove, hand on frying pan, and her husband hunched over the table as he waited for his meal.

He knocked and Mrs. Passingham turned her head. Then putting the frying pan to one side, she wiped her hands on the front of her overall and came to the door.

"I'm afraid this isn't a good moment to come calling," Jameson said with a small, apologetic smile, "but I wanted to catch you before you went out again. The thing is I'd like to have a quiet word with you about certain rumours that are going round the village."

"Rumours?" she said with a frown.

"Concerning one of your employers," he said, casting a quick glance at Mr. Passingham who remained hunched over the table and apparently oblivious of the conversation taking place a few feet away from him.

"It's not very convenient now," Mrs. Passingham said, also giving her husband a quick glance. "We're about to have our dinner. I always give him a hot meal middle day and then he just has a bowl of porridge for his supper."

"If you name a time, I can come back later."

"I'll be home soon after four. About half past'll be all right if you want to come. I'll have him in front of the telly in the other room by then."

"That'll be fine." He paused and, lowering his tone slightly, said, "I expect you can guess what I want to talk to you about."

Mrs. Passingham's upper lip trembled, the only sign of emotion she ever showed, but she said nothing.

When he returned at four thirty that afternoon, she was alone in the kitchen, waiting for him.

He watched her as, without a word, she poured him a cup of tea, added milk and one lump of sugar and put it on the table. He had once had tea in the Wimbles' kitchen and she clearly remembered how he liked it.

She brought her own cup across to the table and sat down at right angles to him.

"What do you want to talk to me about, Mr. Jameson?" she said, with, again, a tell-tale tremble of her upper lip.

9

"It's about Mrs. Wimble. When did you last see her?"

"At the end of September."

"That's almost two months ago. Do you know where she is?"

"Mr. Wimble said she'd had to go all sudden to her aunt's sickbed."

"Do you mean that she was at Downview Lodge one day, but not the next, and you've not seen her since?"

"Yes."

"Had she ever mentioned a sick aunt to you?"

Once more the upper lip trembled in its strangely forbidding way. "No."

"Where did the aunt live?"

"I don't know."

"Mr. Wimble didn't say?"

"No."

"And you didn't ask him?"

"It was none of my business," she said sharply.

"How long had you worked there?"

"Ever since they moved into Downview Lodge."

"When was that, Mrs. Passingham?"

"Four years ago last May."

"And Mrs. Wimble never mentioned any aunt during all that time?"

"I've never said that. She did once or twice mention one who lived in Scotland."

"Did she ever go and stay with her?"

Mrs. Passingham shrugged. "How should I know? It was none of my business."

"But did she ever say she had?" Bob Jameson asked in a faintly exasperated tone.

"No."

"How did you get on with Mrs. Wimble?"

"She always treated me very fairly," Mrs. Passingham replied stiffly.

"I've heard it said in the village that she could do no wrong in your eyes."

The upper lip trembled menacingly. "Some people can't mind their own business," she said scornfully. Then as if uttering her final word on the subject, she added, "Mrs. Wimble's a real lady."

"Do you think anything could have happened to her? That she may have come to some harm?"

"You'd better talk to Mr. Wimble. He's the one to answer those questions."

"Would you have expected her to send you a postcard while she was away?"

Another shrug. "Sometimes she did, sometimes she didn't." She stared into her empty cup. "I've told you all I can."

"I'd like to have your impressions..."

"My impressions are my own business. I don't believe in gossiping. There's too much mischief in the world without adding to it with tittle-tattle."

"I gather Mr. Wimble has had a lady friend staying with him at Downview Lodge?"

"Who he has there is none of my business," she retorted tartly.

"Has he said when he expects his wife to return?"

"No. Come to that, I don't see him all that often. He leaves notes on the kitchen table saying when he'll be down next and if he wants me to get anything in."

Aware of Ada Passingham's reputation, Bob Jameson hadn't expected to be swept away on a floodtide of information. Nevertheless, there was something about her manner which puzzled him. It wasn't so much her customary tight-lippedness as a display of

11

nervous wariness, as if she suspected he was trying to corner her.

He finished his tea, which was by now cold, and pushed his cup away from him. Then fixing her with a steady look, he said, "Do you think there's anything to the rumours that Mr. Wimble has killed his wife?"

"I don't pay any attention to rumours." Her upper lip began to tremble violently and she turned her head quickly away to stare out of the window. A few seconds later she rose from the table. "I must go and see if my husband's all right."

Bob Jameson got up reluctantly. He didn't like being shown the door quite so pointedly. On the other hand, it was clear that he was not going to learn anything further on this visit.

On arrival back at his station, he reported to his sergeant who pursed his lips and told him to have a word with the C.I.D. This meant phoning Detective Sergeant Emmersley who was stationed in the market town of Dinsford about seven miles away.

"Do you want me to put in a report as well?" P.C. Jameson enquired.

His sergeant sighed and repursed his lips. He was close to retirement and invariably chose the softest option, particularly if it relieved him of any work.

"Give Sergeant Emmersley a call and be guided by what he says."

With business thus despatched, he was in the middle of a contented yawn when his telephone began to ring. With a heavy sigh he reached for the receiver.

"There's never any let-up in our job, is there?" he remarked in a pained tone.

Bob Jameson knew and liked Detective Sergeant Emmersley, there not being more than five years in age between them. When he got through to his station, it was to learn that the C.I.D. sergeant was out but expected back shortly when he would be asked to return the call.

"That you, Bob?" Sergeant Emmersley said cheerfully when about half an hour later he rang back. "What's your problem?"

"Sergeant Thrupp suggested I should have a word with you."

Emmersley gave an understanding chuckle and told Bob Jameson to go ahead.

When Jameson had finished, the C.I.D. man said, "I'll be over your way a bit later on so I'll drop by and you can give me the complete run-down on the missing Mrs. Wimble."

It was near enough half seven before he arrived and found P.C. Jameson, who should have been off duty by then, conscientiously waiting for him.

"Pity we can't go and do our business over a pint at the Gander and Goose, but I suppose we'd better not." He pulled a packet of cigarettes out of his pocket and proffered it to Jameson. "Smoke?"

"No thanks, I don't."

"Why do you non-smokers have to sound so smug about it?" he said, glancing round for an ash-tray. "O.K., let's hear it, Bob."

Thus primed, Bob Jameson launched out on a recital of events. When he reached the end, Emmersley remarked, "All you've got is unsubstantiated rumour."

"I know, but I thought I ought to make a few enquires."

"Absolutely right. After all, rumour's the source of a good many investigations. I'd have thought the next step is to confront Wimble." Jameson nodded, but looked nonplussed when Emmersley added, "And you're the obvious person to do that."

"Me?"

"Of course. It'll be much better to keep it low key until we know a bit more. We don't want to go barging in like stormtroopers, only to retreat with egg on our faces. There's no evidence he's killed his wife. We don't even know she's dead. But if you, as the local copper, go along and say there are one or two nasty rumours going around which you think he ought to know about, he'll probably thank you and explain just what has happened to his wife. That way there's no aggro for anyone."

"And if he doesn't come up with a satisfactory explanation..."

"Let me know and we'll decide what further action is called for." He paused. "It's extremely unlikely that he's going to break down and confess to murdering his wife. That being so, one of two things is likely to happen. He'll either give you her address or he'll tell you to get stuffed."

But when, the next day, Bob Jameson managed to track down Wimble's London telephone number, it was to be told that his quarry was in America and not expected home until shortly before Christmas.

"Mrs. Wimble has gone with him," a rather haughty voice informed him.

2

And there the matter rested without further development until mid-December when P.C. Jameson heard on the village grapevine that Frank Wimble was back at Downview Lodge.

Accordingly, at eleven o'clock on a Saturday morning, he turned into the drive of the Wimbles' home and parked his vehicle on the lonely expanse of a vast car port.

He could see Wimble's 3.8 Mercedes, registration number FW 01, sitting in the open garage. It had always surprised him that anyone should want a number that would instantly stick in the public mind. But such was some people's vanity that anonymity in any form became an anathema.

As he walked toward the front door it opened and Frank Wimble came out. Though he had recently celebrated his fiftieth birthday, he could have passed for somebody at least five years younger. He was a well-built man with a golfer's shoulders and a handsome face topped by a head of thick black hair which tended to curl at the back. He was wearing a pair of fawn slacks, a cream-coloured shirt and a black crew-neck sweater.

"I saw you coming up the drive, officer," he said in a tone that was neither welcoming nor hostile. "What can I do for you?"

Bob Jameson glanced around uncertainly. The drive on a grey December morning was no place to conduct the interview he had in mind. It was obvious from Frank Wimble's stance, however, that he was not going to be invited inside the house without first stating his business. If then.

"I'd like to have a word with you, sir, about a somewhat delicate matter," he said firmly.

"We'd better go into the house then," Wimble replied after the merest pause. He led the way inside and motioned Jameson into a small study-like room immediately on the left as they entered the hall.

Though his ears were alert for any sound, the house could have been deserted for all he heard before Wimble closed the study door behind them.

"What is this delicate matter that brings you here?" he asked in a faintly jeering tone.

"It concerns your wife, sir."

"Ah! I thought it might be that. What about my wife?"

"Can you tell me where she is, sir?"

"Unfortunately not." Observing Jameson's expression, he added, "Because I haven't the remotest idea."

P.C. Jameson swallowed. It was not one of the answers he had expected and he felt himself thrown off course almost before the interview had begun.

"Perhaps you could explain yourself, sir," he said suspiciously.

"My wife has left me and I have no idea where she's gone." Frank Wimble's voice had a steely edge as he went on, "She's put me in a position of extreme embarrassment."

"I understood," Jameson said with all the wariness of someone who has inadvertently wandered into a minefield, "that Mrs. Wimble accompanied you on your recent visit to America."

"Ah! That wasn't the Mrs. Wimble you're enquiring about."

"I don't quite follow," Jameson said owlishly.

"That was a lady who is sometimes known as Mrs. Wimble."

"And when you say you've no idea where your wife is..."

"I mean it," Wimble broke in. "I have no idea at all. I arrived back one evening and found she had gone. Cleared out. Vanished."

"Had she taken all her things with her?"

"Virtually nothing."

"You mean, she left all her clothes behind?"

"Apart from what she was wearing, yes."

"Doesn't that strike you as extraordinary, sir?" Jameson asked, assuming his most cross-examining voice.

"Not if she was intending to make a complete break with her past and start a fresh life with a new identity." Observing the P.C.'s incredulous expression, he went on, "I know it sounds fanciful, but I've had somewhat longer to think about it than you have, officer, and it's what I've been forced to conclude."

"And she gave you no clue that she was planning to do this?"

"I didn't have an inkling." He paused and looked thoughtful for a moment. "Maybe I should have, but I didn't."

"Did your wife know about the lady who accompanied you to America?"

"Yes, I'd known her for over a year before my wife left me."

"May your wife have had a lover herself?"

Frank Wimble smiled sourly. "I wasn't aware of one, but I'm beginning to think that she may have."

Bob Jameson decided it was time to produce his trump card and observe its effect.

"Can you tell me, sir, why you told Mrs. Passingham that your wife had been called away to the bedside of a sick aunt?"

Wimble gave him a rueful smile, but didn't appear put out by the question.

"I had to tell her something and so I said that on the spur of the moment to account for Elspeth's absence. I scarcely wanted to say my wife had cleared out and left me, and, in any event, at that stage I didn't know what had happened except that she had disappeared. It seemed the simplest explanation to give Mrs. Passingham when she arrived the next morning."

"Does your wife have an aunt in Scotland?"

"Yes."

"And is she sick?"

"I haven't the slightest idea."

"Have you heard from Mrs. Wimble at all since she left?"

"Just a short phone call about three or four days later, saying that she wouldn't be coming back and I'd never see her again."

"Have you made any effort to trace her, sir?"

"No." Observing Jameson's expression, he went on, "I wasn't sure I wanted her back in the circumstances. As long as she wasn't making any demands on me, I was prepared to live and let live."

18

Bob Jameson scratched his cheek in a thoughtful manner while Wimble watched him with the same faintly superior smile he had worn throughout.

"Are you aware of the rumours going about the village, sir?"

"That I've killed my wife, do you mean?" P.C. Jameson nodded. "Yes, I received an anonymous phone call accusing me of murder."

"And?"

"And nothing!" he said explosively. "I haven't killed her and that's all I can say."

"You realise, sir, I shall have to report all this to my superiors?"

"I've nothing to hide."

"And that we shall probably want to interview you further about Mrs. Wimble's disappearance?"

"I'll be here over Christmas." In a distinctly mocking tone he added, "I assure you that I'm not going to disappear."

3

Police Constable Jameson returned to the station and reported to his sergeant who sighed heavily and said, "Better let C.I.D. know. Be guided by them." After which he went back to polishing his shoes, something he did several times a day.

Detective Sergeant Emmersley, to whom Jameson spoke next, heard him out in silence and then said, "What's your own view, Bob; do you think she lies buried somewhere in the garden?"

"One thing for sure, I don't believe his story that she walked out on him without even taking a toothbrush."

"That does want a bit of swallowing," Emmersley agreed. "But it still doesn't make him a murderer." He paused. "I'm going to headquarters this afternoon and I'll have a word with Detective Inspector Mappin. I know he's on duty today." In a ruminative tone he went on, "I can see that if we don't do anything, the rumours will simply multiply. On the other hand, at the moment we don't even have any evidence of a crime having been committed. We probably ought to get a fully detailed statement from

Wimble, tying him down to times and movements. We can then cross-check it and see if he's slipped up anywhere."

And that is precisely what happened, with the result that by mid-January the police had become convinced of Elspeth Wimble's death and of her husband's complicity in bringing it about.

Just before Christmas Maureen Yates had arrived at Downview Lodge and had been in residence ever since. It was almost as if Frank Wimble wanted to taunt the police and titillate the gossipmongers.

All efforts to discover his wife's whereabouts had come to nought and no trace of her had been found.

Alive or dead, she seemed to have vanished completely.

Downview Lodge was searched from attic to cellar and likely parts of the garden were dug up. But from the amused tolerance with which Frank Wimble had agreed to these activities, the police had realised their quest would be a vain one.

Toward the end of January, by which time Wimble and his mistress had departed for a ski-ing holiday in Switzerland, Detective Superintendent Barty convened a meeting at county police headquarters to review the situation.

"Well, lads," he said, glancing round the assembled company, "what more can we do?"

He was a normally genial, benign man who affected an avuncular attitude toward his officers. Good work was rewarded by praise over a friendly pint of beer, but those who fell short came across another side of his character, one that resembled a farmer descending on a party of picnickers in a field of young wheat.

"I'm bloody certain he's killed her," Detective Inspector Mappin remarked. Nods all round the table greeted this observation. "But I can't see us getting anywhere until we have proof positive that she's dead."

"That's about the top and bottom of it, Pat," Superintendent Barty said. "I reckon all we can do is keep our file open and review the situation every so often."

"Nobody in Little Misten is under any doubt that he's murdered her," Sergeant Emmersley put in. "What's made their eyebrows take off is the brazen way he's installed his mistress at Downview Lodge. Mind you, there are still quite a few ready to accept his hospitality."

"There's never any shortage of free-loaders," Barty remarked. "As to installing his mistress, it's his way of telling the world he has nothing to fear from our investigation. And for the moment he's right."

"I take it you'd agree, sir, that once we discover her body we'll have enough to charge him?"

"Can't answer that until it is discovered, can I, Pat?"

"I mean, assuming it provides evidence she was murdered?"

"Stop trying to get me to sign a blank cheque, Pat! Depends where she's found, how long she's been dead, what was the cause of death and a host of other things. You know that."

"It's always possible that we shall, at best, only find part of her body."

"Are you suggesting that he's dismembered her and buried the bits in different places?"

"It's a possibility, sir."

"So are a lot of other things." Superintendent Barty patted the bulky file that lay on the table in front of him. "What we have here," he said, "is something as savoury as a hibernating bear's crutch, but that's all it is. We'll meet again if and when there's any fresh development." He turned toward Detective Inspector Mappin and gave him a sly wink. "For example, should one of Mrs. Wimble's ears turn up with the crocuses."

It was not, however, one of her ears, but one of her hands, her left hand to be precise, which eventually led to Frank Wimble appearing at Dinsford Crown Court on a charge of murder.

Part 2

1

There arrived a moment a few weeks before his arrest when Frank Wimble refused to see the police other than in the presence of his solicitor, a suave, silky fellow named Graham Tapling who was one of several partners in a West End firm of somewhat flashy reputation.

Mr. Tapling's advice to his client was to keep his mouth shut and say nothing. Accordingly the police, who are not unknown to take a few liberties when dealing with lesser mortals, found themselves made more aware than they wished to be of the rule book and, as a consequence, considerably frustrated.

It was, therefore, with a good deal of satisfaction that, with an assenting nod from the Director of Public Prosecution whose advice they had sought, they made their arrest one morning toward the end of April. Though even this climactic step was robbed of its rougher edge when, by arrangement, Wimble surrendered himself into their custody in the richly carpeted office of his solicitor.

A few hours later that day he appeared before the

local magistrates and, despite an application for bail, was remanded in custody for seven days.

It was a further six weeks before the prosecution was ready to present its case and ask for his committal for trial at Dinsford Crown Court.

Mr. Tapling had lost no time in briefing two counsel for the defence, Mr. Alan Coe, Q.C. and Mr. Stephen Kitter, though only junior counsel appeared at the magisterial hearing. This was because the defence was not proposing to contest the case at the lower court, a decision accepted only with the utmost reluctance by the accused. It had taken both counsel and Mr. Tapling forty minutes to persuade their client that there was not the slightest chance of the magistrates finding he had no case to answer and, in the circumstances, it was far wiser to agree to an uncontested committal and save their ammunition for the trial itself.

In the course of the conference, which was held in prison, Wimble had become so abrasive that, at one point, Alan Coe had offered to return his brief. But Mr. Tapling, who had known his client for much longer than the two counsel had, managed to steer the occasion to an agreed, if not exactly harmonious, conclusion.

The next day he had hurried back to the prison on his own (with the fees he was charging, it was the least he could do) in order to offer comfort and reassurance.

"I promise you, Frank, that you won't find anyone better to defend you than Alan Coe. He's as tough an advocate at they come and he'll fight your case all the way."

"He better had," Wimble remarked ungraciously, before launching out on the topic that obsessed him. "It's a bloody scandal my not being granted bail. Absolutely monstrous keeping innocent people in prison all this time."

"As I've explained to you, I'm afraid it's very rare for anybody charged with murder to be granted bail."

"So you keep on saying, but it doesn't make it any less of a scandal. Once I'm out, I shall take it up with my M.P. It's time the bloody system was changed."

Mr. Tapling nodded soothingly, something he could afford to do in the circumstances.

Thereafter, Frank Wimble, who had not taken kindly to any aspect of prison life, spent the months following his committal for trail chafing at what he regarded as the law's inexcusable delays. As far as he was concerned, a special court should have been immediately convened so that the whole farcical business could be wound up.

On learning that the next sitting of Dinsford Crown Court was not until the beginning of November, he became so angry that even Mr. Tapling had thought it prudent to tiptoe out of harm's way.

Apart from his solicitor, his two most frequent visitors were Maureen Yates and his married daughter Alison, who was twenty-four. She was the younger of their two children and had always been a favourite of her father. Brian, her brother, who was the older by three years, had, on the other hand, never got on very well with him. He lacked most of his father's more aggressive characteristics and didn't make any pretence at sharing his outlook on life. He had written a rather stiff and embarrassed letter shortly after his father's arrest, but had otherwise stayed aloof.

"He's always been a mother's boy," Frank Wimble had said contemptuously when his solicitor had enquired about him.

It was one day toward the end of September, near

enough the anniversary of Elspeth Wimble's disappearance, that Maureen found him in a somewhat reflective mood on her visit to the prison. Normally, he would spend the time inveighing against those whom he considered responsible for his present plight, but not on this occasion.

"As soon as the trial's over, we'll get married," he said.

She gave him a grateful smile, but her expression suddenly clouded over.

"But if the jury find you not guilty, won't that prove she's still alive?"

"Of course it won't. How can it?"

"I don't know. I was just worried for a moment."

"Well, for God's sake don't worry about daft things like that! Elspeth's dead all right, it's just that I didn't have anything to do with it."

"Of course you didn't."

"So you see, by the end of the year I'll have made an honest woman of you."

She gave him another grateful smile. She looked forward more than anything to becoming the legal Mrs. Wimble. She had been waiting over two years and there was still the strain of his forthcoming trial to be faced.

It was about two weeks later that Mr. Tapling arrived with the news that the trial had now been fixed to start on Monday the tenth of November. Mr. Coe and his opposite number had applied that very morning for a date to be set.

"What do you mean, his opposite number?" Wimble asked suspiciously.

"Mr. Donlon. He's leading for the prosecution. I mentioned his name to you some while ago."

"Is he any good?"

"Not as good as Mr. Coe," Mr. Tapling replied, as if comparing soap powders.

"So it could all be over by the middle of the month," Wimble said in a musing tone.

"Let's hope so."

"By the way, what sort of judge have we got?"

The solicitor licked his lips. This was one piece of information he had dreaded to impart.

"Actually, it's Mrs. Justice Gentry," he said with a nervous smile.

"Did you say Mrs.?" Wimble asked incredulously.

"Yes."

"Are you telling me I've got a woman judge?"

"That's right. By all accounts she's . . ."

"Well, you'll just have to get it changed, won't you? I'm not being tried by any woman."

"Actually, it's the jury that tries you . . ."

"I'm not having a woman judge. She'll be prejudiced."

"You've no cause to say that."

"She's bound to be prejudiced because I'm accused of killing one of her sex."

"You're being absurd, Frank. Anyway, there have to be strong grounds before you can object to a judge hearing a case."

"I've just given them to you."

"Calm down, Frank. Mrs. Justice Gentry is a better judge than some of her male colleagues."

"Some vinegary spinster is she?"

"As a matter of fact, she's a widow with grown-up children and grandchildren."

"I still don't like the sound of her."

"Wait till you see her," Mr. Tapling said with an emollient smile. "You'll be surprised."

2

Dame Isabelle Gentry rather liked wearing her judge's robes, not from any sense of judicial vanity, but because they hid her somewhat unstreamlined figure.

She was sixty-one years old and had been on the bench for four years. Widowed at the age of thirty-three, she had resumed practice at the Bar in order to support her two sons through school. Both were now married and to date had provided her with five grandchildren to whom she was devoted.

Her appointment as a High Court judge had been greeted with some surprise, not least by herself, but her competent performance on the bench had quickly silenced any critics. She was sound, without either quirks or pomposity, and she controlled her court with good-natured incisiveness.

She invariably arrived on the bench carrying a capacious black handbag which she swung in the carefree manner of a school satchel, though, in fact, its motion was entirely dictated by her walk which was a mixture of a duck's waddle and the rolling gait of a sailor.

On the opening day of Frank Wimble's trial she was accompanied into court by local dignitaries with whom she exchanged solemn bows before going through the same performance with the assembled counsel. After which she settled into her chair like a hen on its nest and beamed at the clerk of the court as he turned to speak to her. Her large sallow face was made for beaming, when it would give the impression of becoming powerfully lit from within.

When Frank Wimble stepped into the dock, dressed as if he were off to an important business meeting, he gave her a strong, disapproving stare which she accepted impassively. A minute later he had pleaded not guilty in a tight voice and the clerk had begun to empanel the jury.

Mrs. Justice Gentry always took a watchful interest in this part of the proceedings. She felt like a dutiful hostess trying to put strangers at ease in her home. Some judges busied themselves with their papers and scarcely looked up when it was going on, but she considered they lost a psychological trick by so doing.

Looks like a tough schoolmaster of the old type, she reflected as Ralph Hislop took his place in the jury box. If they have any sense, they'll pick him to be their foreman. She was subsequently to learn that the juror in question was a retired headmaster of strong authoritarian views. Next to him sat Edith Norrington, a placid-looking lady of middle years. Then came someone called Peter Floyd, who was already showing small signs of impatience. She reckoned he was somewhere in his mid-thirties. On his other side was Martin Capper, who looked to be not much more than a schoolboy. He had a pleasant, open face and an air of keen interest. Now that the age limit for jury service had been lowered to eighteen, more and more Martin Cappers were performing this high civic duty. Next to him was another woman, Gwen Hackford, whose dark hair was cut in a severe fringe and round whose neck were looped endless coils of wooden beads. The last juror in the front row was Reginald Upham, who looked ill at ease in his dark suit and obviously unaccustomed collar and tie. The judge would like to have been able to tell him to come more comfortably dressed the next day. The woman who took the seat behind Mr. Hislop intrigued Mrs. Justice Gentry by her smile which never left her face and which was to remain in place throughout the trial. Her name, Joyce Stanley, gave nothing away.

The remaining five jurors were empanelled without incident; indeed, no challenges had come from either side.

From their appearance a good representative dozen, the judge reflected with satisfaction.

"Members of the jury," she said, giving them a welcoming beam, "it may assist you in your private arrangements to know that this trial is likely to last several days." The beam intensified. "You'll realise that I can't be more specific than that. The only other thing to say at this stage is to suggest that when you adjourn for lunch, which, incidentally, will be provided for you on the premises, you should pick a foreman who will then be your spokesman. After the lunch adjournment he or she should take the seat in the front row nearest to the bench." She slewed round and gave prosecution counsel a friendly nod. "Yes, Mr. Donlon, I think we're now ready for you to begin."

Michael Donlon had a generally shaggy appearance. His wig looked as if it had been used for scouring saucepans and his gown was wont to slip from his shoulders with the monotonous regularity of a steadily dripping tap.

"May it please your ladyship, members of the jury, I appear for the prosecution in this case with my learned friend Mr. Platman and the accused is represented by my learned friends Mr. Coe and Mr. Kitter." He hitched up his gown on the right side. "Members of the jury, the story which I am about to unfold to you can only be described as macabre. It is a story as ancient, in one way, as the Old Testament itself and as up-to-date, in another, as a modern crime story."

"Roll out the rhetoric," Alan Coe murmured sardonically to his junior.

Mr. Donlon gave his gown a brisk tug on to the other shoulder and went on, "In brief, what the prosecution allege in this case is that the accused murdered his wife because he wished to marry another woman and his wife wouldn't give him a divorce and that he then secretly disposed of her body. It is only right that I should tell you at once, members of the jury, that the body of Elspeth Wimble has not to this day been found. Not the whole of her body, that is. But what has come to light is her left hand which had been severed at the wrist. The flesh had gone, but the bones remained and on one of its skeletal fingers there was a ring. A golden wedding ring, on the inside band of which is engraved *FW to EW 11 July 1953.*" He leaned forward and added in a dramatic tone, "the eleventh of July nineteen hundred and fifty-three was the day on which the accused, Frank Wimble, got married to the deceased, Elspeth Wimble." He paused as if wondering whether to repeat what he had just said, repetition being part of a jury advocate's armoury, but apparently decided against, for he went on, "Human flesh may perish, but gold endures." He cast the jury a look of triumph as though he were personally responsible for this state of affairs. "Members of the jury, Mrs. Wimble disappeared on the twenty-eighth of September last year and has never been seen again. No trace of her has ever been found apart from her left hand which was discovered on the twenty-third of March this year. Discovered by a Mrs. Brackley when out for a walk with her dog in a wood some eight miles from Little Misten where the accused and his wife had their home. The hand was in fact found by Mrs. Brackley's black retriever, Ben, who brought it to his mistress. Where precisely Ben found it, we shall never know, though it's a reasonable inference that it wasn't very far from the spot he dropped it at Mrs. Brackley's feet. I need hardly tell you that the police subsequently searched every square inch of the wood, but to no avail. It therefore seems probable that her body lies buried elsewhere in the general vicinity and that the hand had been dug up, perhaps by some creature of the forest such as a fox, and dropped at the place where Ben found it."

"Some creature of the forest!" Alan Coe muttered scornfully to his junior counsel. "I suppose the rest of the body was eaten at the teddy bear's picnic."

For the past few minutes Mrs. Justice Gentry had been covertly watching the accused to see if she could detect any reaction to prosecuting counsel's recital. His expression, however, gave away nothing. He wore a look of steely concentration, though she thought she observed a flicker of grim satisfaction when counsel mentioned that a thorough search of the area had failed to bring to light any other evidence of his wife's body. As she glanced away and let her gaze go round the small, packed court-room, she couldn't help remembering how not long ago she had helped her grandson, Adam, bury a deeply mourned pet hamster beneath a tree in the garden, only for it to be dug up two days later by a neighbour's dog.

Frank Wimble had been aware that the judge was studying him. He found it grotesque that his destiny lay largely in the hands of this motherly figure who was dressed up like Santa Claus. He was aware that it was the jury who decided the case, but they would obviously take their cue from her and God knows what she mightn't choose to tell them. He, for sure, wasn't taken in by her benign expression.

Although he was the focus of attention, something he ordinarily enjoyed, he found himself chafing at his passive role. He hated just sitting there and listening. He was used to being behind a desk with two telephones constantly ringing and a stream of decisions to be taken. And six months in custody had done nothing to blunt his thrusting nature.

What prosecuting counsel was now telling the jury was not new to him. It was the narration of evidence shortly to be adduced, which was contained in the statements of the prosecution witnesses. Statements which he had read and annotated and been through a dozen times with his solicitor. He had been told, however, that he must still listen carefully to Donlon's opening speech and be ready to make a note of anything that occurred to him. At the moment the pad of paper on the ledge in front of him was still in its virgin state.

The trial was just like a game in which judge, counsel and jury were all going to make their various deductions about what he was supposed to have done. All the prosecution could do was reconstruct while the defence did their best to destroy the edifice thus erected. He believed that he alone knew the real truth, though even that might have been disputed. He was impatient to get into the witness box and tell his story and, although warned that he would face some awkward cross-examination, he reckoned he would be more than a match for the shaggy old bore who was now droning away to the jury.

Donlon had moved on from his summary of the prosecution's case to a detailed recital of the evidence he would be calling. It was a painstaking performance which plainly failed to hold all the jury's attention all the time. In fact, the juror named Floyd, who had exhibited early signs of impatience, was glancing at his watch with increasing frequency, as if he had a train to catch.

Mrs. Justice Gentry rather sympathised with the jury. She had wondered more than once whether it was really necessary for prosecuting counsel always to describe the evidence in such thorough detail. However, having no legitimate cause to interrupt, she was obliged to suffer along with the jury. It was unfortunate, she reflected, that Michael Donlon had such a monotonous delivery. Listening to him was like munching stale biscuits.

He was still on his feet when the court adjourned for lunch. If slow hand-clapping had been in order, she was sure it would long since have broken out.

3

"We'll be here until Christmas at this rate," Peter Floyd remarked in a loud voice as he and his fellow jurors were shepherded into their retiring room where twelve plates of chicken salad met their gaze. "By the way, my name's Peter Floyd."

This led to a general murmured exchange of names, after which Mr. Hislop, the retired headmaster, cleared his throat and said in a gently reproving tone, "I don't think we ought to measure our duty solely in terms of time."

"To me time is money," Floyd retorted. "I'm a sales rep and every day I spend here is costing me hard cash. As a matter of fact I tried to get excused, but they said I didn't come within any of the recognised categories of exemption."

Mr. Hislop turned away as if to register disapproval of such a mercenary approach to jury service.

"Do you think it's all right to start eating?" Martin Capper asked Gwen Hackford. "I got jolly hungry sitting there listening to that counsel."

"I can't say he stimulated any of my appetites," she replied with a harsh laugh. Then glancing around,

39

she said, "Am I the only one who's ever sat on a jury before?"

"Good lord, can it happen more than once?" Reg Upham asked in alarm. He ran a hardware store in a village outside Dinsford and was paying a nephew to mind it in his absence.

"I've known people summoned for service two or three times," Gwen Hackford said airily, at the same time rescuing a piece of lettuce that had become entangled in her beads.

"I'm sure we'll all be glad to have the benefit of your experience," Mrs. Norrington said, slipping into her natural role of family peacemaker. "By the way, is it Miss or Mrs. Hackford? I'm afraid I didn't catch."

"You didn't catch because I didn't say. But since you now ask, I prefer to be Ms. I don't care for these discriminatory distinctions." With a toothy smile, she added, "But I've no objection to anyone calling me Gwen."

She turned to her neighbour on the other side who was the ever smiling Joyce Stanley as if to invite a response. But Miss (or Mrs.) Stanley said nothing and merely went on smiling.

"I wonder if he really did it," young Martin Capper remarked to Peter Floyd. "Fancy cutting up your wife and burying her in bits."

"I really don't think we ought to start discussing the case before we've heard the evidence," Mr. Hislop said firmly.

"But it's what counsel told us," Martin said, with a touch of indignation.

"I don't think he actually said Mr. Wimble had dismembered the whole body," Mrs. Norrington murmured.

"Her left hand had been cut off all right," Martin said defensively. "Counsel said so."

"May I suggest that this sort of discussion is rather premature?" Mr. Hislop broke in. "Now, what could profitably occupy our minds is the election of a foreman. I don't know if there are any volunteers, but..."

He was about to advance his own qualifications when Mrs. Norrington looked toward Gwen Hackford.

"What about you, as you've been on a jury before?"

A suggestion which was met by an annoyed frown from Mr. Hislop, who realised the situation could easily slip away from him.

"I've had a good deal of experience of chairing committees and guiding discussion groups," he said quickly. "If anyone thinks that might be helpful, I'd be happy to serve as your foreman."

"Perhaps you feel it's a male prerogative," Gwen Hackford remarked with an acid smile.

"Of course I don't," he said indignantly.

"It's all right, I was only teasing," she said. Weaving her fingers sinuously through her strands of wooden beads, a sudden look of amusement came over her features. "As we have a female judge perhaps it's only fair that our foreperson should be a man."

Peter Floyd let out a snort of laughter while everyone else assumed tentative smiles.

"That seems to settle that," Floyd said briskly, "you be our foreman, Mr. Hiscock."

"It's Hislop. If that's the general wish..." he said, looking round the table and receiving a series of nods. "All right, I'll be glad to serve." His tone, however, reflected a note of umbrage at the way his election had come about. It had lacked the dignified acclamation he would have regarded as fitting.

"Let's hope things speed up this afternoon," Floyd said, addressing his observation to Joyce Stanley, who smiled her agreement. Or perhaps it was her disagreement.

Meanwhile Martin Capper was eyeing a remaining lump of cheese and wondering if he dared take it. In the end, he did so. It was the first time he had found himself an equal in the company of people most of whom were old enough to be his parents. He was determined to play his part and not let himself be written off as a callow youth whose views hardly counted. To him, jury service held out the prospect of adult fulfilment. He was being given a responsibility accorded to few, namely to decide whether or not a fellow human being was guilty of murder. He was, nevertheless, thankful that the death penalty had been abolished.

4

Mrs. Justice Gentry returned to the bench in a genial mood. She made a point of not eating too much at lunch and eschewed alcohol in any form. It tended to make her feel sleepy and she could remember very clearly, during her early days at the Bar, appearing in front of a dear old judge who invariably dozed off after lunch. Counsel would cough, scrape their feet and even drop large legal tomes in attempts to bring him back to life, but a few minutes later his chin would again be resting on his chest. He was the source of many an anecdote, but Isabelle Gentry had always felt quietly ashamed of an exhibition which could only diminish public confidence in the administration of justice.

As she gave prosecuting counsel a friendly nod to continue his opening speech, she could not help reflecting that he stood in danger of sending her court to sleep.

Fortunately, he showed early signs of reaching an end.

"And so, members of the jury," he said, "I have now outlined to you the case which the prosecution is about to prove through its witnesses. Remember that it is for the prosecution to satisfy you beyond reasonable doubt of the accused's guilt, not for him to establish his innocence. But if, at the end of the day, you are so satisfied, it will be your duty to return a verdict of guilty. My lady will direct you as to the law, but the facts will be for you to determine."

Mrs. Justice Gentry sighed quietly. Prosecuting counsel were always so intent on showing their fair-mindedness, that they were apt to usurp the judge's function. She wished they would stick to their own job and leave the judge to get on with his. But the practice had become too ingrained to eradicate overnight.

"In short, what you have here, members of the jury," Donlon went on just when he had seemed on the verge of sitting down, "is the classic story of a marriage in difficulties, of another woman and of a murder. And who, members of the jury, had both motive and opportunity to commit that murder? The prosecution suggest there is but one answer to that question." He flung out an accusing arm. "Namely, the man sitting in that dock."

This time he did sit down and the court seemed to stir itself into life. Kenneth Platman, his junior, rose to his feet.

"The first witness, my lady, is Bernard Coleman who produced the album of photographs. Neither side has requested his attendance and I beg to read his statement."

Mrs. Justice Gentry nodded her approval and turned toward the jury. "There's a sensible provision whereby witnesses whose evidence is formal and non-controversial are not, subject to the agreement of both prosecution and defence, required to attend in person. Instead their evidence is read out to you.

This first witness took the photographs which you are about to see."

The usher distributed albums of photographs to the jury who opened them with an avidity that would have gladdened the heart of a purveyor of pornography. Several jurors had quickly turned to those showing Elspeth Wimble's severed hand and Mr. Platman had some difficulty in reclaiming their attention.

The first two photographs were estate agent's views of Downview Lodge. There followed two of Wimble's Mercedes, with a third showing an open and capacious boot sufficient to accommodate several bodies. Next came photos of the wood in which Mrs. Brackley and Ben had taken their walk and finally came three of the skeletal hand showing the ring on its third finger. The final photograph in the album was one blown up to show the inscription on the inside band of the ring.

The judge watched the jury with wry amusement. They were just like children with a new picture book. It was their first opportunity to do rather than be, and she was prepared to let them enjoy themselves for a few minutes, at the end of which time they'd be ready to listen again.

The first witness to be called was Dr. Farrer. After eliciting his name and address, Donlon said, "I believe you and your partners carry on a medical practice at Little Misten?"

"We cover a much wider area than Little Misten itself."

"And is the accused your patient?"

"No."

"I'm sorry, I should have said his wife?"

"She was never my patient either," the witness said. "My partner, Dr. Young, used to attend her."

Donlon nodded. "Quite so," he said, as if congratulating himself at having straightened things out. "But I think you know the accused even though he was not your patient."

"I've met him socially on a number of occasions."

"Now I want you to direct your mind to the twenty-eighth of September last year. Did you happen to drive past Downview Lodge?"

"The occasion you're referring to was on the twenty-ninth," the witness said firmly. "About half past one in the morning."

"That would be the early hours of Saturday morning?"

"Yes."

"Spot on at last," Alan Coe murmured to his junior.

"Where were you going?"

"I had been called to visit a patient in Little Misten and was on my way home."

"And what happened when you approached the entrance to Downview Lodge?"

"A car came out of the drive and turned in the direction I was going."

"How far ahead of you was it?"

"About eighty yards when it first emerged on to the road, but it quickly accelerated away."

"Could you see who was driving?"

"No, except that I had the impression it was a man."

"What make of car was it?"

"A Mercedes."

"Did you observe the registration number?"

"It was FW 01," the witness said drily.

"Are you sure?"

"Yes."

"You were able to see it clearly at eighty yards?"

"I was about eighty yards from the drive when the car came out and turned right. I almost caught up with it at that point, but only for a few seconds as it accelerated away from me."

"Do you know where it went?"

"I could see its lights dipping and weaving ahead and it took the left fork half way up Bunyan Hill. I continued on my way toward the London road."

"Do you happen to know where the left fork leads to?"

"It's a meandering lane for about five miles and eventually joins the road which runs west out of Little Misten."

"Do you have any idea where the Mercedes was going?"

"None," the witness said firmly.

"Thank you, Dr. Farrer," Donlon said and sat down.

Alan Coe had not expected to find the doctor easy to cross-examine and his demeanour in the box had merely confirmed this. It was clear that he was not the sort of witness to become rattled under cross-examination. He hadn't said much, but his evidence carried the devastating inference that Frank Wimble had been on a mission to dispose of his wife's body. Any attempt to budge him was likely to boomerang. All this severely limited the possibilities of effective questioning and yet there was the psychological necessity of putting on an act. All this flitted through Coe's mind as he rose to his feet.

"You've told the court, Dr. Farrer, that you knew the accused socially?"

"That is correct. I didn't know him well, but I'd met him on a few occasions."

"May I assume that you knew about his high-powered success in the world of business?"

"Yes, I think it was common knowledge in the district."

"I'm sure it must have been," Coe said with an encouraging smile. "From what you knew of him, would you describe him as a somewhat mercurial person?"

Dr. Farrer appeared to weigh his answer before replying. "Of mercurial habits, perhaps. I'm not qualified to speak of his temperament."

"You mean he was a here, there and everywhere sort of person?"

"He seemed to have that reputation," the witness said warily.

"I'm not trying to catch you out, Dr. Farrer," Coe said with another smile. "Now, you said earlier that Mrs. Wimble was a patient of your partner, Dr. Young?"

"Yes."

"I expect you're aware that the defence will be calling Dr. Young as a witness?"

"So I understand."

"Do you know that he had been treating Mrs. Wimble for her nerves?"

"Yes."

"And that she had been exhibiting signs of strain shortly before her disappearance?"

The witness glanced anxiously toward the judge who turned her own gaze on defending counsel.

"Mr. Coe," she said, "if you are proposing to call Dr. Young, surely he is the right person to whom to put such questions?"

"I entirely agree, my lady, but I thought I'd see if Dr. Farrer could also assist."

"The trouble seems to be that he can do so only by giving hearsay evidence," she said with a small quizzical smile.

"In that event, my lady, I won't pursue the matter any further with this witness," Coe said smoothly, having succeeded in planting what he desired in the jury's mind. He turned back to the witness. "Dr. Farrer, you, of course, had no idea why the accused was out driving in the early hours of that Saturday morning?"

"None. Indeed, I thought I made it clear that I didn't even know it was him at the wheel."

"You did. Most fairly, if I may say so. But, in fact, there's no dispute about who was driving. It *was* Mr. Wimble. For all you knew, he might have been going out to look for his wife?"

The witness was silent for several seconds, then speaking as if his words were especially fragile, he said, "I have no idea where he was going or why."

"And we're certainly not inviting you to speculate," Mrs. Justice Gentry broke in quickly, giving the witness a disarming smile.

"I have no further questions to ask this witness, my lady," Coe said when the judge turned back to him. As he sat down he whispered to his junior, "At least I've trailed a fresh scent under the jury's nose."

Stephen Kitter nodded keenly. He was a capable young barrister and a distant cousin of Mr. Tapling's wife which wasn't the only reason he had been briefed, though it was not a disadvantage when it came to tilting balances.

When defending, Coe always made a practice, during the early stages of a trial, of trying to attract the jury's attention to one of his own points. He felt his questioning of Dr. Farrer had achieved this.

Donlon's next witness was Ada Passingham. She came into court wearing a thick navy blue coat and a black straw hat shaped like an inverted pie dish (it was her only one and was kept for funerals). It was pulled well down as if she were expecting high winds, or even something worse, in court. She took the oath and then looked about her with an air of disapproval.

"Would you like to give your evidence sitting down?" the judge enquired.

"I'll be better standing, thank you," the witness replied stiffly.

"Is your name Ada Passingham and do you live at Peartree Cottage, Little Misten?" Donlon began.

"Yes," she said, with a threatening tremble of her top lip.

"And used you to work at Downview Lodge?"

"I still works there."

"How many days a week?"

"What, now or then?"

"When Mrs. Wimble was there?"

"I did five mornings in those days."

"I want to ask you about the time she disappeared from home. Do you remember when that was?"

"I should do."

"Tell us what you know."

"She was there when I went on the Friday morning. She wasn't there on Saturday."

"Were those the twenty-eighth and twenty-ninth of September last year?"

"If you say so."

"Had you been aware that she might be going away?"

Mrs. Passingham's upper lip trembled uncontrollably at this apparently innocuous question.

"She hadn't said anything about it when I saw her that Friday," she replied after taking a deep breath.

"You know Mr. Wimble, of course. That's him sitting in the dock, isn't it?"

"Yes."

50

"Was he at home on the Friday?"

"I didn't see him."

"And the next day?"

"The Saturday do you mean? He came into the kitchen while I was taking my coat off."

"What time would that have been?"

"Half past nine."

"Did he tell you where Mrs. Wimble was?"

"He said she'd been called very sudden to a sick aunt."

"Did he say when she had gone?"

"He said he'd driven her into Dinsford to catch the last train to London the previous night."

"Did you ever see Mrs. Wimble again?"

"Never seen her since."

"Did you ever ask how long she'd be away?"

"No. It was none of my business."

She threw the accused a look of dislike which also conveyed a suggestion of satisfaction that he was sitting where he was.

"Do you know that he subsequently told the police that his wife had gone away and left him?"

"Yes."

"But did he ever tell you that?"

"Never."

Donlon resumed his seat with a sense of relief. He might have pressed her for greater detail, but he had extracted the vital parts of her evidence. The police had warned him that she was an unwilling witness and he had decided to confine her testimony to its bare bones. He hoped, however, that Coe might experience his own difficulties with her. From the look she bestowed on defending counsel as he rose to cross-examine, it was not a vain hope.

"Am I right in thinking, Mrs. Passingham, that

you used to see much more of Mrs. Wimble than of her husband?" Coe asked blandly.

"He was away a lot."

"So the answer is yes."

"Yes," she said with an ominous tremble of her lip.

"You liked Mrs. Wimble, didn't you?"

"She was a very nice lady," she said with a note of defiance.

"How did you get on with Mr. Wimble?"

"He didn't bother me."

"Do you mean that he didn't interfere with your work?"

"I didn't take much notice of him and he didn't take much notice of me."

"You kept out of each other's way, in fact?"

"You can put it like that if you want."

"Indeed, would it be fair to say that you were a bit wary of each other?"

"It was like I've said," she replied with a frown.

"You weren't on particularly friendly terms?"

"Didn't have to be, did we?"

"Looking back, do you agree that there was nothing surprising in Mr. Wimble not wanting to tell you his wife had suddenly left him?"

"It was up to him."

"Quite so. And you weren't on the sort of terms where you exchanged confidences?"

Mrs. Passingham briskly shrugged away the question as though suspicious that counsel was suggesting something improper.

"Have you not made your point, Mr. Coe?" Mrs. Justice Gentry broke in.

"Probably, my lady. I won't press it further." Turning back to the witness, Coe went on, "What was Mr. Wimble's demeanour when you arrived on that fateful Saturday morning?"

"How'd he look, do you mean?"

"Yes. Did he appear nervous or upset or in any way different from usual?"

"I didn't notice anything special about him," she said guardedly.

She's covering something up, thought Coe. I wonder what it can be?

"When he came into the kitchen and told you his wife had been called away to an aunt's sickbed, did he say anything else?"

"Not as I remember."

"And he seemed quite normal?"

Again a guarded look came over Mrs. Passingham's face.

"I didn't notice anything special," she repeated.

"In the weeks immediately preceding her disappearance, had Mrs. Wimble seemed to be under strain?"

"She told me she was under the doctor with her nerves."

"Did you see any sign of nerves?"

"Some days she talked a lot, others she scarcely spoke."

"Any other signs?"

"She used to go out for long walks by herself."

"How do you know?"

"She called at my cottage one evening and told me she'd been out walking for several hours."

"What time of evening was that?"

"About nine o'clock."

"Was it dark?"

"No, it was summer."

"I'm not allowed to ask you what she said to you about her walks, but did you get the impression that particular occasion wasn't an isolated one?"

"She told me she quite often went for walks," Mrs.

Passingham said, while judge and counsel exchanged resigned glances. Aware of having transgressed, she added crossly, "That was what you asked me, wasn't it?"

"It doesn't matter Mrs. Passingham. It was my fault," Coe said, "I should have phrased my question differently. There's only one other matter I want to ask you about. Do you remember an occasion when Mr. Wimble had cut his finger rather badly on a broken glass?"

"Yes."

"What happened?"

"Mrs. Wimble called me because he'd come over faint. She said he always fainted at the sight of blood."

Donlon lumbered to his feet. "That answer would also appear to be hearsay," he remarked.

"Where was Mr. Wimble when Mrs. Wimble said that?" Coe asked.

"She was holding his finger under the cold tap."

"So he was present?"

The witness glanced about her as if suddenly caught up at a mad hatter's tea party.

"Of course he was if she was holding his finger under the tap," she retorted.

"Did he say anything himself?" Coe asked, ignoring her obvious bewilderment. "He couldn't. He came over faint again," Mrs. Passingham said in a dismissive tone.

"Perhaps I'd better let the matter rest there, my lady," Coe said with a small self-deprecating smile. "I will, of course, be calling evidence of the accused's abhorrence of the sight of blood."

"Thank you, Mr. Coe," Mrs. Justice Gentry observed. Turning to prosecuting counsel, she said, "I think we have time for another witness, Mr. Donlon."

The witness whom Donlon chose to call was Brian Wimble, the accused man's son. Watching him as he took the oath, the judge decided that he might have been the chocolate-box reproduction of a famous painting. The likeness was there, but the quality of the original was missing. He had his father's features without his air of forcefulness.

He appeared extremely nervous and stumbled over the oath. As he put down the testament he cast his father a quick uneasy glance, but Frank Wimble was studiously ignoring him.

"Is your name Brian Wimble and do you reside at the Sidney Savant Hospital in Manchester?" Donlon asked.

"Yes."

"Are you a qualified doctor and a house surgeon at the hospital?"

"Yes."

"When did you qualify?"

"Last Easter."

"Is the accused your father?"

"Yes," the witness said, swallowing uncomfortably.

"What was the last time you saw your mother?"

Wimble closed his eyes for several seconds as though meditating. "It would have been at the beginning of September last year. I came home for a weekend."

"Was your father there?"

"No."

"How did you find your mother on that occasion?"

"Unhappy."

"Do you know the cause of her unhappiness?"

"My father's conduct," he said in a tight-lipped tone.

"How does he know that?" Coe enquired audibly.

"Yes, how do you know that?" Donlon echoed.

"She told me."

"Just as I thought, it's hearsay," Coe observed, rising to his feet. "I don't want to make too much of it, my lady, but as we do have rules of evidence, I would ask my learned friend to try and keep within them."

"Perhaps you both should," Mrs. Justice Gentry remarked mildly.

Coe acknowledged the admonition with a faint smile and sat down.

"Do you remember spending an earlier weekend at home last summer when your father was there?"

"Yes, at the beginning of July."

"Did anything happen between your mother and father on that occasion?"

"There was a quarrel."

"What about?"

"About my mother's refusal to give my father a divorce."

"How did the quarrel start?"

"My father told my mother she was being selfish and unreasonable. When she said she didn't want to go into it all over again, he became very angry and shouted abuse at her."

"Did she shout back?"

"No."

"How did the row end?"

"By my father storming out of the room."

"How would you describe his mood on that occasion?"

Wimble grimaced distastefully. "Savage. He always hated being thwarted by anyone."

"Were you ever present on any other occasion when they quarrelled?"

"No, but my mother told me . . ."

Donlon broke in quickly. "I'm afraid we're not allowed to hear what your mother told you, unless your father was also present."

"He wasn't."

"One final matter, Dr. Wimble. I would like you to look at this gold ring. Do you recognise it?"

"Yes, it's my mother's wedding ring," he said in a terse whisper.

"Are you quite certain?"

"Absolutely. It bears her and my father's initials and the date of their wedding."

It was apparent to Mrs. Justice Gentry that witness and accused were very obviously avoiding looking at each other, which was understandable in the circumstances. Giving evidence was plainly an ordeal for Brian Wimble. His forehead had the sweaty shine of a candle taken from a damp cupboard. He also had dark shadows beneath his eyes, which, themselves, lacked any lustre. Presumably the strain of the past year had taken its toll. It was a cruel experience to be called to give evidence against your father on a charge of murdering your mother. She glanced at the statement he had made to the police, on which his age was recorded as twenty-seven. Even so... If she had been in charge of the prosecution she would have done everything possible to avoid calling him. It was an experience that could scar him for life.

Meanwhile, Donlon had sat down. In his view, it had been necessary to call Brian Wimble as his was the only direct evidence of a hostile motivating spirit on the part of the accused.

Alan Coe came slowly to his feet like a Polaris missile breaking the water's surface in slow motion.

Fixing the witness with a hard look, he said, "You don't like your father, do you?"

Brian Wimble frowned, then swallowed, closed his eyes and screwed up his mouth before replying with

57

a small sour smile, "I think I like him as much as he likes me."

In a tone that plainly told the witness not to fence clever with him, Coe said, "Now perhaps, you will answer my question."

Wimble shrugged. "We've never had a close father-son relationship. I've always been made to feel that he despised me because I wasn't in his mould."

"And you resented that?"

"I just accepted it."

"Would it be fair to say that you were always closer to your mother?"

"Absolutely."

"Were you devoted to her?"

The witness looked momentarily overcome by emotion. "Yes," he said in a half-whisper.

"I take it that you were on her side in the quarrel about which you told the court?"

"Certainly I was. My father was in the wrong."

"Because he wanted a divorce in order to be able to marry another woman?"

"Yes."

"Did you never consider he was entitled to some understanding?"

"Not on this particular issue."

"And yet he and your mother remained together for over twenty-five years?"

"Largely because it was my mother who made all the concessions."

"You're not suggesting she wasn't in love with him?"

"No, because I know she was."

"Am I right in saying that the only contact you've had with your father since his arrest last April has been one letter which you wrote to him in prison?"

"Yes."

"In effect, you've abandoned him?"

"He'd mentally abandoned me long before that," Wimble said sharply.

"What I have to put to you is that you are so filled with resentment toward your father that you tend to exaggerate anything which will show him in a poor light. Is that right?"

"No."

"I suggest that the row which took place the weekend you were at home was nothing like as serious as you've described; that, in fact, it wasn't much more than a normal domestic disagreement?"

"It happened as I've described."

"Did your father ever, to your knowledge, use violence toward your mother?"

"No."

"I imagine your mother would have told you if he had?"

"Probably."

"So we may assume he never did?"

"He had this funny thing about violence. He couldn't stand the sight of blood."

"Ah!" Coe said in a voice that positively pounced, "I was about to ask you about that. It's true, isn't it, that he was apt to faint at the sight of blood?"

"Certainly at the sight of his own blood. If he cut himself, for example."

"Was he not equally squeamish at the sight of other people's blood?"

"Not to the same extent. But then he could usually avoid looking."

"Has he always been like that?"

"For as long as I can remember. He was useless if my sister or myself ever needed a bit of first aid as children."

"Would you consider him capable of cutting up a body?"

Brian Wimble gave defending counsel a curiously shrouded look. "No way," he said.

It was, Coe decided, the right time to sit down.

"We seem to have reached a suitable moment to adjourn," Mrs. Justice Gentry said with an approving smile. Turning toward the jury, she went on, "Members of the jury, we'll adjourn until ten thirty tomorrow morning. In the meantime, may I suggest that you don't discuss the case outside the walls of the jury room. So far you've only heard part of the prosecution's case and, of course, nothing of the defence's. It's therefore important that you should keep an open mind and, in particular, not allow yourselves to be influenced by anything you may happen to read in the newspapers about the case." The candle power of her smile increased. "Your families and friends may want to hear your first-hand impressions, but I suggest you avoid getting drawn into any detailed discussion or expressing any view. You can tell them what I have said."

She rose, exchanged bows with counsel, gave the jury one to itself, and, picking up her large black handbag, departed from the bench with a swinging gait.

5

When Mr. Tapling went down to the cells beneath the court to see his client, he found him sitting on a wooden bench, legs thrust out and on his face a look that summed up his feelings about the day he had spent in the dock. A look compounded of frustration, resentment and raw anger.

"I know how you're feeling, Frank," he said, "but it's all going as well as we could hope." He produced a packet of cigarettes from his pocket. "Have a smoke. It'll help ease your nerves."

"Isn't it usual for counsel to come and see their client at the end of the day?" Wimble asked in a grating tone. "Or aren't I paying them enough?"

"Alan Coe had to get back to London urgently, but he told me to say he'd have a word with you before the court sits in the morning. He's quite satisfied with the way things are going. He felt he'd made some good points with both Mrs. Passingham and with your son."

"Brian's as wet behind the ears as the day he was born," Wimble said in a tone of disgust.

"I don't think he much enjoyed being in the witness box."

"I should bloody well hope not. At least it'll be different when Alison gives evidence. She's on her father's side all right."

"What's more, I don't think Brian made a very good impression on the jury," Mr. Tapling remarked in a bedside manner.

"I don't like the look of that female who's covered in beads," Wimble said viciously. "I know she's already decided I'm guilty. She keeps on glowering at me."

"I'm sure you're mistaken, Frank. On the whole they appear a good sound jury."

Wimble let out a snort. "Bugger your good sound jury. I want one that'll say I'm not guilty." He paused and scowled at the opposite wall. "The foreman looks like a sour old bank manager who's spent his life refusing overdrafts to widows. As for that woman with the silly smile..."

"Calm down, Frank. You're letting your imagination take flight. You can rely on Mr. Coe to fight every inch of the way and he's got a whole lot of tricks up his sleeve which he's waiting to play."

Frank Wimble gave his solicitor an abstracted look. All he hoped was that fate hadn't any more tricks up her sleeve to play on him.

6

Gwen Hackford lived on her own in a flat on the outskirts of Dinsford and had done so since her husband had walked out on her three years earlier. Driven out (according to his version of their breakup) by her uncompromising feminist views. Views which had become increasingly reflected in her various attitudes toward life and which finally soured their marriage.

According to her, however, the blame lay in his obvious lack of sympathy with emanicipated womanhood.

She was now secretary of the local branch of the Achievement of Women's Rights Association and it was to the monthly meeting of the Association that she was bound at eight o'clock that evening.

The first thing she did on arriving home from court was make herself a cup of herbal tea. Armed with this, she sat down to relax for a while, first browsing through the latest issue of the Association's quarterly magazine, then checking the minutes of the previous month's meeting which she would be required to read out to the assembled membership. Thereafter she fell into contemplation of the day she had just spent in court.

She regarded her summons to jury service as a call to civic duty, and she was nothing if not civic conscious. On the other hand she had no doubt that the law still discriminated against women. Female judges were a move in the right direction, but they were as few and far between as sultanas in an economy cake. Morever, she had heard of barristers' chambers that blatantly refused to accept women and it was noticeable that there was always a preponderance of men on juries. It occurred to her that this might be a fruitful subject for research with a view to an article in her Association's magazine.

Her mind drifted on to a consideration of the particular case she and her fellow jurors had been empanelled to try. It seemed most unlikely that the prosecution had been able to unearth the whole truth (unearth was the right word!) and the sole concern of the defence would be to confuse, obfuscate and lay false trails. It was the system which was at fault; it simply wasn't designed to elicit the truth. It could only have been created by men.

As for the man they were trying, he was obviously full of masculine self-esteem. Nobody who read newspapers could help knowing something about Frank Wimble and his millions. He was not the sort of man with whom she could ever have any empathy.

Though she would, of course, keep an open mind until she had heard all the evidence, she didn't have much doubt that he had killed his wife and disposed of her body with the brutal lack of concern of a one hundred percent male chauvinist.

Mrs. Hislop thought her husband looked tired when he arrived back from court.

"Sit down, dear, and I'll fetch you a cup of tea," she said. Her life was dedicated to his well-being, something he had long accepted as a matter of right.

"I confess I do feel a bit weary," he said, handing her his hat and coat to hang up. "It requires full-time concentration sitting on a jury."

"Is it an interesting case?" she enquired.

"It's that millionaire chap, Wimble, who's alleged to have murdered his wife."

"Is that the one where all they ever found of her was her hand?" He nodded and his wife gave a small shiver. "I don't think I'd like listening to all those gory details. Are you enjoying it?"

"Enjoyment doesn't enter into it. It's a matter of doing one's duty to the best of one's ability," he said in a sententious tone. "Incidentally, I've been elected foreman of the jury."

"They obviously recognised you as a natural leader," his wife said with a note of pride. "Did they know you'd been a headmaster?"

"Yes, I mentioned it when we were discussing who should be foreman. It seemed important that some-one suitable should be picked. You need somebody with a bit of authority."

"Let me get you your tea, dear, and then you can tell me all about it," his wife said as she hurried off to the kitchen.

But when she returned a few minutes later bearing a tray, he said, "I'm afraid there's nothing to tell. The judge warned us not to discuss the case with anyone while it was in progress."

"Not even with your wife?"

"Not even with you, dear!"

"But what harm could it do?"

"It's important that I keep an absolutely open mind."

"And telling me about it might prevent that?" she asked, incredulously.

"I might be influenced by something you said."

It was a possibility they both knew to be absurd.

When Peter Floyd arrived at his office after that first day in court, he immediately embarked on a flurry of telephone calls and dictated memos to persuade himself that he was recapturing at least some of the time he had lost.

His new secretary, Anthea, supplied by an agency, seemed quite willing to work late. It was her first job after leaving secretarial school and she had been considerably impressed by the aura of high-powered activity her employer generated about him. She also found him rather attractive after a succession of somewhat callow and immature youths of her own age.

At seven o'clock, as he signed his last letter, he said, "Go and do what you have to do and I'll take you out for a drink."

She raised her eyebrows in faint surprise. "Won't your wife be expecting you home?" she asked.

"I'll phone her while you're getting ready. We might even have a meal as well."

After she had gone out of the room, he put through a call to his wife.

"Sorry, sweetheart, but I'm still stuck in the office trying to catch up with things. I definitely won't be back for supper so don't wait for me. I'll nip across the road later for a sandwich."

By the time he rang off, Anthea was standing in the doorway with an expectant expression.

"Do you want to phone anyone before we go?" he asked, looking her up and down with distinct approval. This was her first week and he'd hardly had an opportunity to register her finer points.

She shook her head. "I'm not expected home till ten anyway."

"Oh! Who are you throwing aside for the pleasure of my company?"

"I've signed up for French evening classes. It won't hurt to miss one."

Peter Floyd grinned. "Fine! Then let's go and I'll tell you what it's like being on a jury."

"Well, what is it like?" she asked some twenty minutes later when he returned from the bar with the sweet Martini she had asked for and a large Scotch for himself.

They had gone to a newly opened steak house five miles out of town and were seated in its brightly lit cocktail lounge.

"What is what like?" he asked, closing the gap between them on the banquette.

"Being on a jury, of course," she said.

He shook his head slowly in a gesture of despair. "It's so drawn out, you could scream with frustration. You'd think all the counsel were on overtime the way they spin it out."

"What sort of case is it?"

"Murder. That chap who killed his wife and buried her body."

"How creepy! Why'd he do it?"

"He wanted to marry someone else and his wife wouldn't give him a divorce."

"He's not that man who lived at Little Misten?" she asked in an excited voice.

"That's him."

"My mum has a cousin who lives there so we've heard all about it. He sounded a horrible man."

"His wife may have been a bit of a shrew."

"Even so, to kill her and then bury her body."

"I agree, it is going a bit far."

"I can't see you ever doing anything like that," she said with a coquettish smile.

He grinned. "There's a world of difference between wishing it and actually doing it."

"Aren't you happily married then?" she asked in a speculative tone.

"Oh yes, but one gets an itch from time to time."

"Isn't it supposed to be every seven years?"

"I reckon my next major one will be in ten years time when I'm in my mid-forties."

"Are you thirty five? You don't look it."

"Thirty-four as a matter of fact. How old do I look?"

She studied his face for a few moments in silence. "You don't really look more than thirty-one or thirty-two."

"Oh!" he said in a deflated tone. "You wouldn't put me still in my twenties?"

"Not really! How old is the man who's killed his wife?"

"Fifty."

"How long will they keep him in prison?"

"He hasn't been convicted yet."

"But he did it, didn't he?"

"You bet, but it's a question of whether the prosecution can prove it."

"Do you mean he might get off even though he did it?"

"Happens all the time," he said, with an air of authority.

"My grandfather thinks they ought to bring back hanging."

"A lot of grandfathers hold that view."

"Have you got a crusty old judge like the ones on T.V.?" she asked after a pause.

"As a matter of fact, it's a lady judge. She's rather an old dear."

"What about the other jurors, what are they like?"

He grimaced. "A motley bunch if ever I saw one. There's one not any older than you by the look of him and another at the opposite end of the age scale who's a retired schoolmaster and as starchy as they make 'em. There are a fair number of nonentities. Oh, yes, and a women's libber, all beads and hair in a straight fringe. I reckon she'll be tiresome when it comes to considering our verdict. Come to that, I can see one or two of them proving difficult."

"How do you mean, difficult?"

He grinned. "Not agreeing with me."

"But you said just now you didn't know whether he'd be proved guilty or not."

"True. But you're unlikely to get twelve people all agreeing, whichever way it goes."

"Your view may be wrong," she said, giving him a teasing glance.

"I may be in a minority, but I shan't be wrong," he remarked, watching her to see whether she laughed. But she didn't and he went on, "Let's have another drink and then we'll talk about something more interesting. Such as you."

"Give us another kiss," Martin Capper whispered into the ear of his girlfriend Debbie.

"Oh for heaven's sake, stop all your whispering and waggling your heads about," said an exasperated voice from the seat behind. "Some people want to watch the film."

Debbie let out a nervous giggle while Martin turned and glared at the small, elderly man in the seat behind who had spoken.

A little later Martin and Debbie moved to the end of the row where they were able to sit in comparative isolation.

"It's a rotten film anyway," he said as they started to kiss again.

After leaving the cinema, they bought fish and chips and walked back to Martin's home, where they knew they would have the sitting-room to themselves. His father being away on business, his mother would have retired to bed on the dot of ten o'clock. And his two younger brothers would also be in bed and asleep.

Martin worked as a draughtsman in an architect's office and was enjoying this, his first job since leaving the school where he and Debbie had originally met at the age of sixteen. Or more accurately, that was the age at which they had begun to show an interest in one another.

Debbie was currently working in a boutique and had aspirations to become a model, though everyone told her she was much too short. In any event she was beginning to think that a job on the local newspaper might be more to her liking. She had visions of being an intrepid young reporter. It would be more exciting than being a model. Also she wouldn't have to watch her diet so carefully.

"Fancy old Hislop being on your jury!" she said, as she and Martin sat on the sofa eating their fish and chips. "Do you think he recognises you?"

"Not him. He never taught me and my face was just one of eight hundred in general assembly."

"Are you going to tell him you were at Stanbridge High?"

"I might do. Depends."

"You never liked him, did you?"

"Did anyone? He was just a remote figure who had no use for anybody except the scholarship types. As far as the rest of us were concerned, we were fodder on a conveyor belt and the sooner we fell off at the other end, the better." He was lost in thought for a moment. "I suppose the real reason I didn't like him was because he wasn't fair. That time he cancelled a half-holiday for everyone because somebody had written 'Ayatollah Hislop' on a wall. You'd have thought high treason had broken out the way he reacted. He was a sanctimonious old hypocrite and I bet he's still the same."

Debbie laughed. "I'd love to see his face if you do remind him you were at his school. I mean, you and he serving on the same jury together."

Martin nodded. "And where my vote is just as good as his. I bet he'll try and get everyone round to his way of thinking, but he'll find it a bit different from the classroom."

"I'd like to see him try and bully you, Martin," Debbie said, happily.

"I'll tell him where he gets off if he does try."

He slowly licked each of his fingers in turn and then wiped them on his handkerchief. "I'll go and make some coffee."

"Shall I come and help?"

"Of course, you know I can't boil the kettle on my own."

When they returned to the sitting-room Debbie said, "How long will the case last?"

"The judge said several days. By the way, did I tell

you it's a female judge? She's rather motherly. Not a bit like you'd imagine."

Debbie tried to picture herself as a judge but failed.

"What about the defendant, what's he look like?"

Martin's expression clouded over.

"I'm not meant to discuss the case with anyone. The judge told us not to."

"I don't see why you can't tell me what the defendant looks like. That isn't giving anything away. After all, I could have been in court and seen him for myself."

Confronted by this piece of irrefutable logic, Martin gave way.

"Do you remember that Member of Parliament who came to prize giving our last year? He looks a bit like him."

Debbie frowned as she sought to conjure up a mental picture. Suddenly she exclaimed, "Of course I remember him now. He was the person Carole Sutter wrote to afterwards asking for a signed photograph. He replaced Robert Redford as her number one pin-up."

"He didn't look anything like Robert Redford."

"I know, but Carole thought he looked a real dish of manhood. She always did fancy older men."

"This chap's fifty," Martin observed, as though referring to someone on the verge of senility.

"I wonder if he did it," Debbie said. "Killed his wife, I mean."

"It's too soon to know," he said firmly. Then with a worried frown, he went on, "I'll tell you one thing, though. His son was called to give evidence against his father and I didn't like that. I mean, what a thing to have on your conscience."

"Perhaps he didn't have any choice."

"I'm sure he could have got out of it somehow if he'd really wanted to. I couldn't see myself ever giving evidence against my dad, even if he killed my mum."

Debbie shivered. "I'll have nightmares if you go on like that."

"You started it."

"I know I did, but now let's talk about something different."

"I have a better idea. Let's not talk at all," he said, as he pulled her into his side and began nuzzling her neck.

Joyce Stanley was still wearing her smile, as if it were a piece of permanent make-up, when she got back to the "Old People's Home" where she was employed as a cook. It was, indeed, her front to the world at large.

"Am I glad to see you back, Joyce!" exclaimed Mrs. Parker, the warden, who came hurrying into the kitchen at the same moment as Joyce entered through the outside door. "That young assistant of yours is worse than useless on her own. In the end I couldn't bear it any longer and packed her off to her room. She'll have to go as soon as I can get a replacement. I really can't be doing with her. On top of everything else, she turns sullen every time I speak to her. Anyway, thank goodness you're back."

"I have to go to court again tomorrow," Joyce said, smiling.

"Oh, no! I thought it was for only one day."

"Probably be four or five. Even six."

"Well, really!" Mrs. Parker expostulated. "There must be hundreds of people with nothing better to do whom they could put on their juries, but they have to take our one and only cook."

The warden flounced out of the kitchen, watched by an unmoved Joyce, who recalled how, when the jury summons had come, she had been thrown into near panic.

In the first few moments of shock she felt certain it was a trap of some sort; or that her past had been deliberately resurrected to test her.

But after a cigarette and two cups of tea her nerves had calmed down and she had realised that the summons had no sinister import. It merely meant that her name had come out of a hat or been spewed forth by a computer whose job it was to select jurors.

Thus reassured, she had read the document through with care. There was a bit to tear off and sign and return to somebody and she didn't want to make any mistakes.

There was something in the explanatory notes, however, that caused her smile to fade and be re-placed by a worried frown. It informed her that any-one who had been sentenced to life imprisonment or to a term of five years or more was disqualified from sitting as a juror.

She read and re-read this sentence several times, wondering if it applied to herself.

There was nobody she could ask: or, more pre-cisely, it was not a question she had any intention of asking anybody. She must decide for herself whether or not it was applicable to her circumstances.

Eight years had gone by since she had stood in the dock at Liverpool Crown Court and been sentenced to life imprisonment for the murder of her husband. But then there had been the appeal when her con-viction and sentence were quashed and she had sud-denly found herself free. Her solicitor had been at pains to explain to her that the effect of the Appeal Court's judgment was the same as if she had never been found guilty and sentenced.

That must mean she wasn't disqualified from being a member of a jury.

Eight years since she had stood in the dock charged with murder, six and a half since she had changed her name to Joyce Stanley and moved south. For the first three years she had lived in London, then spent the next two in Canada. On her return to England she had taken up residence in Dinsford, which she had first noticed out of a train window. She had felt that a medium sized country town, not too far from London, would best suit her.

Her smile, vacuous and at times unnerving and exasperating to others, was the legacy of a nervous breakdown she had suffered when the whole business of her trial and appeal was finally over.

As she had contemplated the jury summons, she had realised it had been sent in all good faith. And it was in all good faith she had signed the form acknowledging that she would attend Dinsford Crown Court on the day instructed.

After all, why shouldn't she serve on a jury? She would probably know more about what went on than most of her fellow jurors, for, though large portions of her past life had become lost in an amnesic fog, she had a peculiarly clear recollection of her trial.

And now here she was with the first day over and, Mrs. Parker notwithstanding, looking forward to the remainder of her service. Though she had not attempted to make any contact with her fellow jurors, apart from turning her smile on them, she felt she was very much one of them.

Reg Upham's nephew greeted the return of his uncle with an exhaustive (and, to Reg, exhausting) account of everything that had happened during the day while he had been in charge of the shop. He was a humourless and self-opinionated young man whose favourite topic of conversation was himself. He showed a minimal interest in everything else.

As he talked he began buckling on his motor cycling gear, watched by his uncle who reflected that he might have been about to undertake a journey into space, such was the complexity of his apparel. When Reg had ridden a motor cycle all you needed was a flat cap and a pair of goggles.

It was only after his nephew had departed in a throaty roar of sound that it dawned on Reg that at no point had his nephew asked him anything about his own day in court.

In view of the judge's strictures, that was, perhaps, as well. Even so it would have been agreeable to have been given the opportunity of rebuffing his interest.

As it was, he had nobody to talk to or listen to until his nephew returned at eight thirty the next morning.

Edith Norrington was one of those women for whom the description of "housewife" had been designed. It never bothered her thus to describe herself on any official form she was required to complete. It fitted her as deftly as a kitchen apron.

Her husband, who was a bank manager, had shown a lofty condescension toward her summons to jury service, as he did toward most of her activities.

"All I can say is, rather you than I," he had remarked. "Personally, I can't think of a greater waste of time." The fact was he felt considerably galled at not having been summoned himself.

As soon as she arrived home from her first day in court, she disappeared into the kitchen to prepare dinner.

While she was there, she heard the front door open and close a number of times indicating the return of her family from their various labours.

Apart from her husband there was Anthony, her twenty-year-old son, who was articled to a firm of chartered accountants, and Clarissa, aged eighteen, who was studying art at a local polytechnic.

With one ear she listened to the comings and goings on the far side of the kitchen door. On one occasion she was aware of a muffled phone call taking place.

But nobody so much as poked a head into the kitchen to see how she was or to enquire about her day. It was enough for her family to know that dinner was in the process of preparation and would, in due course, arrive on the dining-room table.

And when the four of them did eventually sit down to their meal, it would be her role to listen and, where necessary, attempt to mediate. She didn't expect any of her family to seek her opinion, any more than she expected it of her fellow jurors.

7

The letter from the Lord Chancellor saying that he was thinking of recommending her appointment as a judge of the High Court had come as a complete surprise to Isabelle Gentry. Moreover, it had thrown her into considerable confusion.

Inevitably she felt honoured and flattered, but, at the same time, alarmed by the prospect of all the panoply that accompanied a High Court judge on circuit, the travelling from town to town, being greeted and entertained by local dignitaries, who would also turn up to bow her in and out of court.

Since her children had grown up, she had lived alone in a small flat which overlooked Hyde Park. She did all her own cooking and enjoyed giving small dinner parties over which she took enormous trouble. Twice a week a Spanish woman came in and cleaned, leaving the place smelling strongly of garlic and lavender polish.

Her sons, with whom she had discussed the Lord Chancellor's letter in confidence, were in no doubt that she should accept.

"Think how you'll enjoy having your grandchildren at your installation, or whatever the ceremony is," John, her elder son, had said.

The thought had caused her to smile and though it seemed a frivolous consideration in such a weighty matter, it nevertheless stuck in her mind.

When one or two of her closest friends at the Bar gave her similar advice, backed up by more long-term reasons, her last doubts were overcome.

In the event, she had thoroughly enjoyed her first four years on the bench. There were evenings when she longed to be alone in her flat in London, which, apart from weekends, she often didn't see for long periods on end. On the other hand, the presence of a hired staff in the various judges' lodgings had its agreeable side. In particular she enjoyed the luxury of a chauffeured car to transport her to and from court. Standing in bus queues and fighting her way into the Underground had never been favourite pastimes.

When she arrived back at the judges' lodgings in Dinsford (a wing of a Queen Anne house on the outskirts of the town which was owned by the National Trust) she decided she had time to bring her notes up to date before getting ready to go and have dinner with the High Sheriff.

This was something she made a point of doing each evening. The more complex the case, the more vital the task. She was aware that many of her friends thought of her as having a delightfully easy life, sitting from ten thirty to around four thirty. Few of them realised how much homework a judge had to do if the job was to be efficiently performed.

Reading through her note of the evidence in the Wimble case, however, would not take her all that long. It was a matter of underlining various parts and making a cross reference in the margin where different witnesses testified as to the same incident.

Though every word spoken in court was taken down by a shorthand-writer or by mechanical means, it had always been the custom for judges to make their own note of the evidence. Thanks to her own brand of shorthand, Mrs. Justice Gentry could keep up with the fastest talking witness and rarely had to have anything repeated. It was a feat much appreciated by counsel appearing in front of her.

As she settled down to work, the butler brought her a tray of tea things and she poured herself a cup. Very different from the tea-bag and quick "cuppa" she would have, were she at home.

She had just finished her labours and had decided she still had time for a pleasant read before going upstairs to change for dinner when the butler reappeared to tell her that she was wanted on the telephone.

"It's Mr. Peter Gentry, my lady," he said, holding open the door for her.

Peter was her younger son. He lived near Winchester, had a wife named Fran and two children, Adam aged ten, whose pet hamster's obsequies she had assisted at, and Jane aged eight.

She was looking forward to spending the coming weekend with them and, as she made her way to the small room at the opposite end of the wing where the telephone was situated, assumed that her son's call was in connection with the arrangements for her visit.

"Hello, Peter," she said cheerfully as she picked the receiver up from the small red velvet cushion on which it nestled. "I was going to call you tomorrow."

"I'm afraid something dreadful has happened, mum," he said in a voice that caused her heart to skip a beat. He had always been the same, either on top of the world or at the bottom of its deepest well.

"To one of the children?" she asked, trying to keep her own sudden anxiety under control.

"No. It's Fran."

"Has she had an accident?"

The question popped out automatically, as she had always regarded her daughter-in-law as a fairly reckless driver and it was a reasonable assumption in the circumstances that she had smashed up both herself and her car.

"She's left me," Peter said in a hollow tone.

"Left you, darling?"

"Yes. I found a note when I got home this afternoon."

"What about Adam and Jane?"

"They went to a party after school. I'm about to go and fetch them home."

Dame Isabelle let out a silent sigh of relief. At least Fran had not taken them with her.

"But where's she gone, Peter?"

"To her parents to think things out," he said in a tone of gloomy resignation.

"But why? What's gone wrong between you?"

"We've had a bit of a bumpy patch this last month or so." He paused, then blurted out. "The truth is, mum, she's met someone else. Someone with whom she believes she's in love."

"Who is he?"

"He's a widower whose children go to the same school as Jane. We first met him at a parents' meeting."

"How old is he?"

"About the same age as me."

"Oh dear, oh dear!" Dame Isabelle said with a heart-felt sigh. The trouble with young marrieds today was that they often seemed to lack staying power. They had no determination to make things work. Moreover, if they did feel any sense of shame or guilt, it was not sufficient to deter them from their waywardness. All these thoughts sped through her mind before she spoke again. "What did she say in the note she left you?"

"She just said she had gone home to her parents to think matters out and wasn't sure when she'd be coming back, but would keep in touch. She reminded me that Adam and Jane would need collecting from their party and that it was the au pair's afternoon and evening off. Oh yes, and she apologised."

Very civil of her, Dame Isabelle was almost stung to say, but didn't. At least her daughter-in-law hadn't vanished into thin air like Elspeth Wimble.

"What about the weekend?" she asked. "Do you still want me to come?"

"Adam and Jane will be terribly disappointed if you don't. Also, if you're here, mum, I may seize the opportunity of going to see Fran. We've got to thrash this out face to face sometime."

"Very well, you can expect me on Friday evening." She paused and in a solicitous tone went on, "Try not to become too depressed, darling. From what you've said, it could be no more than a temporary down in the general ups and downs of marriage. Incidentally, what are you going to tell the children about Fran's absence?"

"I've already thought of that. I shall say she's been suddenly called away to her mother's sickbed."

As long as you don't say it's her aunt's, I don't mind, Isabelle Gentry thought.

8

Mrs. Justice Gentry didn't radiate her customary benevolence when she arrived on the bench the next morning, which was hardly surprising in view of the restless night she had passed. She had been haunted by the thought of Peter and his temporarily motherless children.

"Looks as if she had a drop too much of the High Sheriff's port last night," Coe murmured to his junior. "She's very fond of port, I'm told."

Stephen Kitter's smile turned into a guilty blush as he became suddenly aware of the judge casting him a speculative look. He and Coe had spent the preceding half hour visiting their client in the cells, a visit which had left him smarting from the manner in which Frank Wimble had contrived to ignore his presence.

"I call Professor Penny," Donlon announced.

Raymond Penny was one of the country's most famous forensic pathologists. His name had long been a household word in the criminal courts and latterly he had become a television personality which had brought him still wider fame. He was a short, thick-set man with a shock of snowy white hair and an aura of omniscience.

He reached the witness box and gave Mrs. Justice Gentry a small bow which she acknowledged with a gracious smile. He was fond of relating how, when she was still at the Bar, she had succeeded in non-plussing him by her cross-examination in a particular case. The story, as he told it, was intended to reflect credit on them both. On her for her forensic skill and on himself for acknowledging occasional fallibility.

"Is your name Raymond Penny and are you a registered medical practitioner and a professor of pathology?"

"I am."

"Is your address 335 Harley Street, London, W.1?"

"It is."

"Perhaps I needn't trouble to elicit all your medical qualifications," Donlon said, glancing doubtfully from witness to judge.

"I think Professor Penny is sufficiently well known," Mrs. Justice Gentry remarked, to the witness's obvious approval.

"I'm obliged to your ladyship." Turning back to the pathologist, prosecuting counsel went on, "On the twenty-fourth of March this year, did you examine a hand?"

"Yes."

"Was it the hand shown in photograph seven of exhibit one?"

"It was."

"What can you tell the court about it?"

"It is a female left hand, which has come from a woman of medium build, and it has been severed at the wrist joint. It consisted solely of bone, the nails having dropped off and all the skin and soft tissue having been eaten away. On its fourth finger was a wedding ring."

The witness was handed Elspeth Wimble's ring and, after examing it gravely, identified it as the one he had found.

"How long would it have taken for the hand to have reached the state in which you found it?"

"That would depend on the conditions to which it had been subjected. On examination, I found elements of soil adhering to the bones which indicated that it had been buried in the ground. In addition to soil, I found traces of leaf mould which gives rise to the inference that it had been a shallow burial. In those circumstances, it wouldn't have taken more than a week or ten days in warm, damp weather for the skin and soft tissue to have been completely eaten away. Allow twice that time for burial in colder, drier weather."

"So that after, say, six months burial you would certainly not expect to find any skin or flesh left on the bones?"

"Not if buried in the ordinary ground."

"What in fact would cause the destruction of the skin and soft tissue?"

"Rats, beetles, maggots," the witness replied blithely. "They'd soon pick the bones clean."

The jury seemed to give a corporate shudder at this observation. They had been listening to the evidence with expressions that ranged from clinical interest to unadorned awe. Even Peter Floyd's air of impatience had been replaced by one of absorption. Joyce Stanley had kept her smile intact and Martin Capper could, from his expression, have been watching a particularly good horror movie.

After a few more questions, Donlon sat down and

Mrs. Justice Gentry let out a silent sigh. In her view, prosecuting counsel had failed to ask a lot of questions that required asking and she hoped that Alan Coe might fill some of the gaps. If not, she would have to do so herself before the witness left the box.

"You refer to this hand having been severed, professor," Coe said, as he and the witness faced one another like a couple of familiar contestants. "What exactly do you mean by that word? For example, had it been cut off or might it have separated from the body in the course of normal decomposition?"

The witness had been nodding energetically while the question unfolded itself, as though bursting to answer.

"One thing I'm quite sure about," he said, "it had not been removed with surgical precision. It had either been crudely detached by a knife or similar implement *or* it could have been bitten off by an animal. In my view, it would not have become separated from the rest of the arm without the application of some external force."

"What sort of animal do you have in mind?"

"A fox or a dog."

"The dog that found it, for instance?"

"I don't see why not."

"Except that a thorough search of the vicinity failed to reveal any further parts of the body."

The witness shrugged. "That's hardly a matter of medical science. It's not for me to theorise, but it could have been removed by a fox and dropped at the place where the lady's dog found it."

"You've obviously subjected the hand to exhaustive examination?"

"I have, indeed. I have x-rayed it and tested it for protein cells in the marrow of the joints."

"As a result, are you able to assess the age of the person from whom it came?"

"All I can say is that it is an adult hand. There was no evidence of any form of rheumatic disease in the joints, from which I would infer that it was not the hand of a very old person. It could have come from someone, a woman that is, between the age of thirty and fifty."

"Perhaps, even, as old as sixty or seventy?" Coe said in a coaxing tone.

The witness pursed his lips. "It would have to have been an exceptionally well preserved seventy-year-old," he replied crisply.

"Did you find evidence of the dog's saliva on it?"

"Yes. I had been given a control sample of Ben's saliva and it matched the traces found on the hand. I should add that the tests were conducted in my laboratory."

"Did you find traces of any other animal's saliva?"

"No."

"What do you deduce from that?"

"Either that the hand had not been picked up by another animal or,"—here the witness paused to add weight to his words—"that it had been long enough ago for all such traces to have vanished."

"Were there any other indications of the hand having been carried in an animal's mouth?"

"None."

"Assume for a moment, professor, that the hand had been deliberately cut off, is it reasonable to suppose that the rest of the body has been dismembered?"

"Not necessarily."

"Are the victims of murder usually cut up in order to facilitate the disposal of their bodies?"

"Yes, I think that's a fair inference."

"And in such cases, would particular care be taken to dispose of those parts by which the body might be identified?"

"Yes."

"Such as the teeth and the hands?"

"Yes, though there may be other equally identifiable parts."

"The hands, of course, because of possible identification by fingerprints?"

"Exactly."

"Do you not, therefore, regard it as very curious that, *if* the hand had been deliberately cut off after the victim's death to frustrate identification, a gold wedding ring was left on one of its fingers? And not just any gold ring, but one which revealed even more clearly than fingerprints whose hand it was?"

"It's certainly a puzzling feature, though not strictly one for a medical expert to speculate about."

"Would you not agree, however, that it rather negatives any suggestion of the hand having been detached in order to prevent identification?"

"Has anyone actually made that suggestion apart from yourself, Mr. Coe?" Mrs. Justice Gentry enquired with a faint smile. "My impression is that you yourself put up the suggestion and that you are now busy disposing of it."

"I thought, my lady, that the prosecution was inviting the jury to draw such an inference."

He glanced at Donlon who heaved himself to his feet with seeming reluctance.

"It is for the jury to draw such inferences as they see fit from Professor Penny's evidence," he said with a touch of asperity.

The judge turned toward the witness. "It seems to me, Professor Penny, that you are being drawn into a realm of pure speculation. All you can testify to is the hand which you examined and subjected to various tests. As there is no evidence as to what has happened to the rest of the body, you can't really help the court about what condition it might be in, if it ever were to be found."

"I quite agree with your ladyship," the witness said.

"In due course," she went on, "the jury will have to decide whether the death of Mrs. Wimble has been proved to their satisfaction. That is one of the first issues they will have to consider. The whole question of death and cause of death is inevitably one of inference, there being no direct evidence apart from the hand." She now swivelled round to look at Alan Coe. "I'm sorry to have interrupted you, Mr. Coe, but I felt we were straying rather far from what is helpful to the jury."

"I apologise if I've been guilty of that, my lady," Coe said smoothly, "I was merely trying to make the point that if this body had been dismembered to frustrate identification, it seems very curious that her wedding ring was left on her finger."

"*If*, Mr. Coe, *if*. We have no evidence of dismemberment, apart from the discovery of the hand, which, as Professor Penny has said, is itself open to more than one interpretation. So shall we leave it at that?"

"If your ladyship pleases." Addressing himself to the witness, defending counsel said, "Can you give the court any estimate as to how long the hand had lain buried?"

It was at this point that Mrs. Justice Gentry found herself once more gazing at Brian Wimble who was sitting near the back of the court. He had been listening to the witness's evidence with apparent absorption, at times frowning and at other times looking almost apprehensive, as if fearful of what the witness was about to say. She had not expected to see him back in court after completing his own evidence and she now decided that his experience in the box could not have been as traumatic as she had supposed.

Professor Penny delicately massaged the tip of his nose before replying to Coe's question.

"Assuming it had been buried in a shallow grave of soil and leaf mould, I would say, from the tests I have made, approximately six months, give or take a month either side."

"You're aware that Mrs. Wimble disappeared at the end of September and that the hand was found at the end of the following March?"

"So I understand."

"The condition in which you found the hand was therefore consistent with burial for that length of time?"

"Entirely."

Coe nodded thoughtfully. "It follows from what you have said, but, perhaps I should put it to you explicitly. Are you quite unable to say how the person concerned came by her death?"

"I have no basis on which to form any opinion at all as to that."

"She might have died of natural causes?"

"Yes."

"Or as a result of an accident?"

"That also can't be excluded."

"Thank you, professor," Coe said and sat down.

Mrs. Justice Gentry thought she was able to detect the line of Coe's defence, even though it had only been hinted at. For reasons of his own, he obviously didn't wish to unveil it fully until the moment of his choosing.

Having no questions of her own to ask the witness, she gave him the sort of smile exchanged by busy colleagues in an officer corridor.

The next witness was a railway official from Dinsford station who testified that nobody had joined the last train to London on the evening of the twenty-eighth of September in the previous year for the very good reason that it had been cancelled and didn't run.

As Wimble had already admitted to P.C. Jameson that he had lied to Mrs. Passingham in telling her that he had driven his wife to the station to catch the train in question, Mrs. Justice Gentry was mildly surprised when Coe rose to cross-examine. She couldn't see what benefit it would bring him.

"When did the police first ask you to recall that particular evening?" Coe asked.

"I think it was about the middle of December, sir," the witness replied, with the same flustered air he had worn since arriving in the witness box. Courts were as far removed from his normal world as mediaeval torture chambers and he viewed them both in much the same light.

"That would be about ten weeks later?"

"Something like that," the witness said, glancing about him as if for a bolt hole.

"And did you immediately recall what had happened that evening?"

"Not likely. I told 'em I couldn't remember anything about the evening. It was only when I checked up back at the station, I found she'd been cancelled."

"She being the last train?"

"That's right."

Coe sat down with a faintly peeved expression.

He knows he'd have done better to leave the witness alone, Mrs. Justice Gentry reflected. But sometimes even the most experienced advocates can't resist the siren call to hear their own voices at work on a witness. Fortunately for him his intervention hasn't actually harmed his client's cause, merely rubbed a bit of shine off his own reputation.

There followed a brisk succession of witnesses, each of whom contributed his mite in helping the prosecution to prove that Frank Wimble had murdered his wife.

There was an air of general relief when one o'clock came and with it the lunch adjournment.

9

Not even the smoked salmon sandwiches his solicitor had brought him for his lunch could lift Frank Wimble's spirits off the floor.

It had been a dreadful morning, starting with the meeting he had had with his legal advisers when he had been at his most ungracious. Not that he had ever regarded graciousness as a virtue to be practised, nor had he ever been one to apologise for his personal behaviour.

He wasn't sure what he had expected to come out of the conference, but it had left him as disgruntled and frustrated as it had found him.

Frustration was, perhaps, the key word in describing his condition. After a lifetime of aggressive activity in which he had always sought to assert his control over events, it was almost more than he could bear to sit in court and be impotent to exercise any power over what was going on.

Listening to Professor Penny's evidence had been the turning of a knife in an already sensitive wound. Though he had known in advance what the pathologist was going to say (the prosecution having served on the defence copies of the statements of all the witnesses they were proposing to call) he had been filled with a mixture of resentment and bitter frustration as he heard his counsel and the witness discussing in their urbane manner matters which affected him so vitally.

For the thousandth time he cursed the ill fortune that had so capriciously brought Elspeth's hand to light. It was nothing less than a piece of freakish bad luck which still rankled with him as deeply as the day when the police had told him of the discovery. Since then there had been the constant gnawing fear of what else might suddenly appear. It was no consolation that the police had given up searching for her body, for if an animal had been able to find her hand, presumably another animal might unearth other parts. If ill fortune had seen fit to take one swipe at him, she would be quite capable of another. And there was absolutely nothing he could do to protect himself as long as he remained in custody.

The sword of Damocles had been hanging over his head for more than six months, but each day that passed with it still suspended was no guarantee that it might not fall the very next day.

No wonder, then, that he was filled with anxiety, despair and frustration. No wonder, either, that he regarded his trial as a great big charade in which, perforce, he was a participant.

There were moments when he longed to stand up and shout at them all and say how bored he was with their theories and speculation. Instead of which he was obliged to play along with their rules in order to have any hope of survival.

He bit into his last sandwich. They might all have been filled with pink gelatine for the pleasure they had given him.

* * *

When the police told Ada Passingham that she need not return to court the next day unless she wanted to come as a spectator, she had replied that that was her last wish.

Nevertheless, as she now stood watching her husband slowly masticating his food, she couldn't help wondering what surprises, if any, the morning session had brought.

She would be glad when the whole thing was over. It had brought her nothing but worry and anxiety. She hoped that Mr. Wimble would get his deserts and that would be the last she ever heard of him.

Out of the corner of her eye, she became aware of someone hurrying past the kitchen window. A moment later, there was a knock on the outside door.

"Hello, Mrs. Passingham," Brian Wimble said when she opened it.

"Oh, it's you," she remarked, with a faint tremble of her upper lip. "Do you want to come in?"

"Good morning, Mr. Passingham," Brian said as he stepped inside. But the figure at the table went on slowly eating and didn't look up.

"If you want to talk, we'd better go into the front room," Mrs. Passingham said. Glancing toward her husband, she went on, "He doesn't take in much these days, but you never quite know. Just a minute, I'll pour him another cup of tea. Would you like one?"

"I'd love one. I mustn't stay more than ten minutes as I want to get back to court."

"Has your father's lady friend given evidence yet?" she enquired in a contemptuous tone.

"I think she'll probably be called this afternoon. That's why I want to get back in time."

"What about your sister?"

"I've not seen Alison anywhere around. She's a defence witness and probably won't be called for another couple of days. My father'll be giving evidence before she does."

Mrs. Passingham let out a sniff of general disapproval. Turning to her husband, she said, "Mr. Brian and I are going into the front room for a bit of talk. Call out if you want anything."

He gave a slow nod and went on pursuing an elusive pea round the edge of his plate.

"Old Professor Penny looks just like he does on telly, doesn't he?" Martin Capper remarked to Reg Upham as they made their way to the jury room and lunch.

Mr. Hislop, who was walking immediately ahead of them, turned his head to give Martin a reproving stare.

Stupid old fart, Martin thought. Staring at me as if he were still a headmaster.

"They'd be able to identify me by my bunions," Reg Upham observed equably. "I've got a couple of beauties, one on each foot."

"Hope the professor's evidence hasn't put you off your lunch, Gwen," Peter Floyd said to Ms. Hackford as they processed into their room.

"Why should it?" she asked belligerently. "It's a stupid fallacy to imagine that women are more squeamish than men."

"Glad to hear it," he said in a determinedly bored tone. "Oh, God, it's cold chicken again," he added with dismay as he glanced at the food awaiting them.

"I'm very fond of cold chicken," Mrs. Norrington said in her peacemaker's voice. "At least it's more wholesome than something out of a tin. Don't you agree, Mrs. Stanley?"

Joyce Stanley gave a small nod as she continued to smile.

As soon as they were all seated, Mr. Hislop coughed to call for silence.

"Perhaps while we're having our lunch," he said, "we might have a preliminary exchange of views on the evidence we've heard so far. In order that we don't all talk at once, may I suggest that you let me, as your foreman, call in turn on those who have something to contribute."

"I didn't take to Brian Wimble," Gwen Hackford said immediately. "I thought he had a shifty look about him."

"I felt sorry for the poor young man," Mrs. Norrington broke in, before being frozen into silence by Mr. Hislop's minatory frown.

"Well, I certainly wouldn't want him as my doctor," Gwen retorted. "There was something definitely evasive about him. Don't tell me I was the only person to notice!"

Mr. Hislop rapped the table with the handle of his knife.

"We shall never have a fruitful discussion if we interrupt each other and all talk at once," he said sternly.

"I'd have thought a free for all was just what we did want at this stage," Martin Capper said.

Mr. Hislop compresssed his lips into a thin disapproving line.

"If I may say so, sir," he said coldly, "I doubt whether you've had as much experience as I've had in running discussion groups."

Peter Floyd gave Martin a wink. "So stuff that up your chimney," he murmured.

"It must have been a terrible ordeal for him giving evidence against his father," Mrs. Norrington remarked. "I can imagine how my son would feel in similar circumstances." Aware of a number of surprised glances directed at her, she blushed. "Oh dear, what have I said? I didn't mean to imply that my husband might murder me..." She laughed uncertainly and lapsed into an embarrassed silence.

"Does anyone else have any comment to make on Dr. Wimble's evidence?" Mr. Hislop asked, making another effort to control the discussion.

"I agree with Gwen," Martin Capper said. "There was something about him I didn't care for."

"May I suggest," Mr. Hislop broke in, "that we should be more concerned with his evidence than with his personality?"

"You can't separate the two," Gwen retorted. "If somebody strikes you as shifty, then you hesitate to accept what they tell you."

"I would like to take you up on that, Ms. Hackford," the foreman said. Unable to bring himself to address her as Gwen on a mere twenty-four hours acquaintanceship, he was obliged to fall back on what he regarded as the lesser of two evils, namely the pronunciation of Ms. "Even a self-confessed liar is capable of telling the truth and shouldn't be automatically disbelieved. And Dr. Wimble certainly doesn't fall into the category of self-confessed liar."

"If his evidence is corroborated," she said with an air of authority, "all well and good. Otherwise I shall need considerable persuasion before I accept what he's said."

"It didn't seem to me that he said very much," Peter Floyd said, without waiting for their foreman's green light. "I'm beginning to think we'd do better to postpone any discussion until we've heard all the evidence."

Several jurors nodded and Mr. Hislop assumed a

judicial air. "It wasn't meant to be a detailed discussion so much as a preliminary exchange of views. I thought I'd made that plain. However if you'd prefer..."

"I propose we leave all our arguing until the end," Floyd interrupted. He let out a breezy laugh. "God knows we're going to have enough of it then from all the signs. I can't see us lot reaching an easy agreement." He sighed. "If only somebody could crank a handle and speed things up. I don't know about the rest of you, but it's not doing my business any good sitting here day after day. God knows when we'll get away."

Mr. Hislop had been showing signs of increasing displeasure. He was not used to being interrupted, still less to being contradicted and forced to listen to a lot of brash talk.

"I take it," he said in a glacial tone, "that it's your general view we should defer our exchange of views until the case has got somewhat further."

"I'm not trying to prevent people exchanging views," Floyd said. "It's just that I'm not in favour of a chaired discussion at this stage."

"I agree," Gwen said.

Once more there were a series of nods round the table, leaving their foreman looking as chuffed as King Canute facing the waves.

A few minutes later, with lunch finished, he rose and walked round to where Joyce Stanley was sitting.

"Everything all right, Miss Stanley?" he asked a trifle awkwardly.

She nodded and for a second her smile became alive and something less of a fixture.

"We're lucky to have such an interesting case," he went on conversationally. "It might have been a heavy fraud. Not that I wouldn't have found that interesting, too," he added, to indicate the breadth of his interest. "I take it you've never sat on a jury before?" She grimaced and shook her head. "Or probably even been inside a court?" At this, she gave him such a sharp look that he felt momentarily nonplussed.

He had been privately speculating that deafness might be the reason for her fixed smile and that it was a façade behind which she sheltered. But she had obviously heard what he said without any difficulty. If, on the other hand, he had discovered she wasn't hearing anything that was going on in court, he would have regarded it as his duty to bring the fact to the notice of the judge.

He was now inclined to write her off as someone with a brain the size of a pinhead who would be a complete passenger in all their deliberations.

He was relieved of any further attempts at conversation by the arrival of the jury bailiff to take them back to court.

Isabelle Gentry was particularly thankful that she had the judge's lodgings to herself that lunchtime, apart, that is, from the household staff.

At the busier towns, there would often be two judges, the male one with an accompanying wife, not to mention an attendant marshal.

A marshal was not an obligatory member of the judge's entourage and she didn't have one with her at Dinsford. More often than not, he was a young barrister whose duty it was to sit beside the judge in court and look attentive, and, outside court, to combine the qualities of social secretary and companion for all moods.

On the whole she regarded marshals as an anachronism, but she had yielded to persuasion and had invited a pupil in her old Chambers to join her at the next town on the circuit.

When she was eating alone, she always made it clear to the staff at the lodgings that she wanted only the lightest of meals.

Her first act on arrival back for lunch that day was to put a call through to her son's office. The sudden eruption of his marital difficulties had never been far from her thoughts that morning and it had required a conscious act of will to concentrate on the case she was trying.

On learning that he was out to lunch with a client, she put down the receiver with a resigned sigh, then found herself deriving a measure of relief from the fact that he was doing something so normal. At least it must mean that his world hadn't collapsed any further.

She wondered whether he had told John, his older brother, what had happened. She had meant to ask him when they were talking the previous evening, but, like much else, it had gone out of her mind.

John and Peter had always been close to one another, even though their respective wives viewed each other without great enthusiasm.

She wished she didn't have a number of members of the Bar coming to dinner at the lodgings that evening. On the other hand her sense of duty would never have allowed her to cast everything aside on account of a family crisis.

After all, what was Peter's crisis compared with that of the man she was trying? Though it wasn't a thought that exactly comforted her, it did help to keep matters in perspective.

10

If the prosecution could have avoided calling Maureen Yates as one of its witnesses, Donlon would certainly have done so. The prospect of a difficult witness always made him nervous and there was no doubt in his mind that the accused's mistress was a potentially difficult one, though the police had assured him that she would come up to proof, if only reluctantly.

The reason he felt obliged to call her was simply to prove her relationship with Frank Wimble and thereby provide in its most positive form a motive for his wishing to be rid of his wife.

When the police had first interviewed her and obtained a signed statement, they had acted both with speed and a certain craftiness so that she had committed herself on paper before all the implications sank in.

Nevertheless, it was obvious that her sympathies lay with the defence and that she would agree with everything put to her in Frank Wimble's favour.

She was an attractive woman in her early thirties and came into court wearing a charcoal grey suit over a burgundy red cashmere sweater. Her dark hair was loosely pulled back into a demure bun.

She took the oath in a low voice and faced Donlon with an air of calm confidence.

In answer to his initial questions, she gave her name as Maureen Yates and her address as a flat in Chelsea.

"How long have you known the accused, Miss Yates?" he asked.

"Just over two years. And I'm Mrs. Yates, but divorced from my husband."

"I'm sorry…"

She accepted his muttered apology with a small, supercilious smile.

"Did you know Mrs. Wimble, the accused's wife?"

"I'd met her," she replied coolly.

"What was your relationship with the accused?"

She raised a faintly mocking eyebrow.

"I was his mistress."

"When did you become his mistress?"

"A few weeks after we first met."

"Used he to stay with you frequently at your flat in London?"

"Yes."

"And did you on a number of occasions accompany him to functions and on business trips?"

"Yes."

"Was marriage ever discussed?"

"Frequently."

"In what way?"

"In what way!" she repeated as if ridiculing the question. "We very much wanted to get married, but his wife refused to give him a divorce."

"A divorce on the ground of his adultery?"

"Yes."

"That meant you would have to wait much longer

103

before the marriage could be dissolved on other grounds?"

"So I understood."

"Did this annoy him?"

"We both found it unreasonable."

"Were any alternatives to divorce ever discussed?"

"I wasn't aware there were any alternatives," she replied.

"Mrs. Wimble's death must have come as something of a godsend?"

Coe sprang to his feet. "My learned friend really mustn't cross-examine his own witness," he exclaimed indignantly.

Mrs. Justice Gentry nodded. "I'll ignore that question, Mr. Donlon."

Prosecuting counsel hitched his gown back on to his shoulders and sat down. The witness's quiet self-assurance had got under his skin so that the taunt had slipped out. However, she had said as much as he had expected and had made no attempt to renege on her evidence.

For defending counsel cross-examining such a witness was like a child being given free run of a sweet shop and Coe was ready to indulge himself.

"Is it still your intention, Mrs. Yates, to marry Frank Wimble as soon as that becomes possible?"

"Yes."

"However long you may have to wait?"

"Yes," she said, flashing the accused a sudden smile.

"Are you very much in love with one another?"

"Very much."

"Did he ever at any time mention the possibility of murdering his wife?"

"Never."

104

"He never even hinted at it as a way out of the impasse?"

"Never. I happen to know he couldn't have murdered her."

"Why is that?"

"Because he not only couldn't stand the sight of blood, but any form of violence would make him physically sick."

"We've heard from his son how he would feel faint if he cut himself."

"It's true. He had this complete revulsion at the sight of blood."

"And of violence, too, you said?"

"Yes."

"And that's why you don't believe he'd be capable of committing murder?"

"I'm convinced of it."

"His wife was last seen alive on Friday, the twenty-eighth of September. Where were you that day?"

"In London."

"When did you first know about her disappearance?"

"Frank phoned me from Downview Lodge that Saturday morning to say he'd arrived home late the previous evening to find the house empty. He said his wife hadn't been home all night and he was worried that something had happened to her. He added that their cleaning woman would be arriving any moment and he proposed to explain Elspeth's absence by saying she had been called away suddenly to a sick relative."

"Did he say what he thought might have happened to her?" Coe asked.

"Yes. He knew she'd recently been taking lonely walks after dark and he thought she might have become ill or had an accident while she was out."

"Did he say whether he had looked for her?"

"Yes. He said he'd gone searching for her in his car sometime after midnight, but quickly realised how futile it was seeing that he had no idea where to look."

"That was what he told you on the phone on Saturday morning. When did you next see him?"

"He drove up to London that evening."

"How did he appear?"

"He was worried and, at the same time, angry."

"Did he express any fresh view about her disappearance?"

"He said he was beginning to wonder if she might not suddenly have gone off and left him. It had occurred to him that there might be another man in the background."

"With whom she'd run away, do you mean?"

"Yes."

"Did he mention the question of reporting her disappearance to the police?"

"He said he was going to wait a few days in the hope of hearing from her."

"And did he hear from her?"

"Yes. She phoned him three or four days later and confirmed what he had begun to suspect, namely that she had left him for good and he would never see her again."

"That's what he told you she'd said?"

"Yes."

"What was his reaction?"

"He was stunned." She threw him a quick affectionate glance. "He's never been very sensitive to what's going on inside other people and he was taken completely by surprise."

That's a delicate way of describing an egomaniac, the judge thought to herself.

"Did he say anything further about going to the police?" Coe enquired.

"He said there was no point in doing so as she was alive and well."

"Do you know whether he made any efforts himself to try and trace her?"

"When he realised that the police suspected him of killing her, he inserted notices in a number of papers asking her to come forward and confirm she was still alive."

"What was his reaction when the police told him his wife's hand had been found?"

"I wasn't there when he was told."

"No, but when he next spoke to you?"

"He was completely shattered by the news."

"Like someone whose crime has suddenly found them out, do you mean?"

"Certainly not. He was . . . well, he was shattered, as I've just said. He couldn't believe it. After all, for six months he had lived with the belief she had gone off and left him. Consequently, evidence of her death came as a tremendous shock to him." She paused and bit her lip. "Do you want me to go on?" she asked.

Coe flashed her a speculative glance before saying firmly, "No, I think we'll leave it there, Mrs. Yates."

It had occurred to the judge that the witness was, in effect, giving a preview of what the accused was going to say when he came to give his evidence. As she now saw the defence taking shape, she couldn't hold back a professional's respect for its artfulness and ingenuity. It was clear that every twist of the accused's conduct would be plausibly accounted for, though it remained to be seen to what extent the jury swallowed his explanations. But that was looking some way ahead and, meanwhile, the prosecution was not without its own difficulties when it came to proving its case. She foresaw that much might eventually hang on the effectiveness of Donlon's cross-examination of the accused, on the outcome of which, however, her hopes were definitely muted. Cross-examination was such a linchpin of the accusatorial system that, if incompetently conducted, it could leave the jury with a lopsided, even false, picture of events.

Coe decided that he had got all he wanted from the witness and, after a whispered word with Mr. Tapling in the row behind him, resumed his seat.

Donlon at once indicated that he didn't wish to re-examine the witness. Indeed, as the purpose of re-examination is to attempt to restore a witness's credibility after it has been dented by cross-examination, the question didn't arise. Perversely, Mrs. Yates's credibility had been actually enhanced by cross-examination and there was nothing he could do about it. It niggled him, however, that he had been obliged to call her for the prosecution.

The next witness was Police Constable Jameson who testified to visiting Downview Lodge on a grey December morning in order to interview the accused about his wife's disappearance.

He had never given evidence in the Crown Court before and he experienced a quiver of apprehension when Coe stood up to cross-examine him. It was all very different from facing one of the known local solicitors in a case of "drunk and disorderly" before a bench of lay justices.

"Am I right in thinking that you were the first of several officers to interview the accused?" Coe asked.

"That is so, my lord," Jameson said, suddenly recalling that he should address his evidence to the judge. "I mean, my lady," he added quickly with a furious blush.

108

Mrs. Justice Gentry decided to save him further embarrassment by pretending not to have noticed.

"When you saw him that Saturday morning, did he appear furtive or evasive?"

"No-o."

"Not like somebody who has something to hide?"

"No-o."

"Each of your noes, officer, has managed to convey doubt. If you have any doubts, let us hear them. Do you?"

Jameson shook his head unhappily. He felt he ought not to be agreeing with defending counsel and, in any event, because Wimble hadn't appeared furtive or evasive didn't mean he hadn't murdered his wife.

"No," he said.

"The truth is, officer, that he was remarkably frank with you, wasn't he?"

"In what way, sir?"

"When you put to him the explanation he'd given Mrs. Passingham for his wife's absence, did he not immediately confess to you that it was a lie and say why he had told it?"

"Yes."

"Are you suggesting, Mr. Coe," the judge broke in, "that what he then told this witness represented the truth, namely that his wife had left him?"

"That was what my client believed to be the truth at the time, my lady," Coe replied suavely.

"Thank you, Mr. Coe, I just wanted to be clear," the judge said in a tone to match counsel's.

Coe turned back to the witness. "Am I right in thinking it was village gossip that caused you to go and see the accused?"

"Yes."

"Did you tell him that?"

"Yes, sir, I said to him, 'Are you aware of the rumours going round the village?' and he replied, 'That I've killed my wife, do you mean? Yes, I received an anonymous phone call accusing me of murder.' He then added that he hadn't killed her and that's all he could say."

"Nothing could be much franker than that, could it?"

"That's not for me to say, sir."

"Do you think, officer, you could try and be as frank with me as the accused was with you?" Coe said sharply.

"I'm answering your questions as best I can, sir."

Defending counsel gave the jury a long-suffering glance in an attempt to enlist their sympathy.

"Were you present when the house and garden at Downview Lodge were searched?"

"On two occasions, sir."

"Was every room, cellar, attic and cupboard searched for clues to Mrs. Wimble's whereabouts?"

"Yes, sir."

"And every outhouse, too?"

"Yes."

"And nothing whatsoever was found?"

"Nothing."

"Was every square inch of the garden dug up?"

"Not dug up, sir."

"Probed with rods then?"

"Yes."

"And were certain areas also dug up?"

"Yes, sir."

"And is it within your knowledge that searches were also made of fields and woods in the vicinity?"

"Yes, sir."

"All to no avail?"

"I wasn't in charge of the operation, sir."

110

"I'm well aware of that, but you know the outcome of all those searches?"

"Yes, sir."

"Which was that not a single clue was found to indicate what had happened to Mrs. Wimble?"

"So I understand, sir."

"And did the accused cooperate fully in all those searches?"

"Detective Superintendent Barty will be able to answer that better than me, sir."

"Did the accused ever try and obstruct the police in any of their searches?"

"No, sir, but as I've just said..."

"I'm aware of what you've just said," Coe said gratingly. "I accept that you are not the officer in charge of the case, but that doesn't mean you can't answer my questions."

"But it does mean, Mr. Coe, that he is not the best witness to whom to put them," the judge broke in. "Why don't you wait until Detective Superintendent Barty is in the box?"

"Is your ladyship directing me not to put these matters to this witness?" Coe asked with an edge to his tone.

"You know quite well, Mr. Coe, that I'm doing nothing of the sort. I'm merely suggesting that the officer in charge of the case is the more appropriate witness of whom to ask such questions."

Three further police witnesses completed their evidence before the court adjourned for the day, leaving Detective Superintendent Barty as the only prosecution witness remaining to be called.

11

On leaving court, Floyd offered Martin Capper a lift.

"My car's in a yard at the back of the building," he said as they reached the pavement. He led the way round the side of the court-house to an entrance, on one of whose pillars was a notice in heavy black letters.

"Private. No Parking. Court Officials Only."

"I hope your car's still here," Martin said with a grin.

"It'd better be, if they want to see me again tomorrow. I was damned if I was going to leave it in the municipal car park and walk half a mile as I did yesterday. I haven't got the time to be buggered about by petty bureaucracy. After all, we're a darned sight more important than any court official."

"What happens if a juror does refuse to turn up?"

"I don't know and I don't really care," Peter Floyd said. "If they tried any funny tricks with me, I'd raise hell."

Martin thought it much more likely that he, Floyd, would be on the receiving end of any hell that was going. He had it at the back of his mind that a judge could confine recalcitrant jurors in the dungeons and, at the very least, impose fines on them.

For all Peter Floyd's brashness Martin found him more of a kindred spirit than any of the other jurors. He secretly admired his refusal to kowtow to authority or to be overawed by the panoply of the law.

When they reached the car, they found it as it had been left and without any abrasive notices stuck on its windscreen.

As they drove out of the yard, Floyd said, "I must say I took quite a fancy to Maureen Yates. Wouldn't mind having her as my mistress. That is, if I could ever afford one," he added with a laugh.

"She was a bit too mature for my taste," Martin remarked. "But I thought she gave her evidence very well."

"You sound as if you're awarding her points for deportment and voice production."

"What I meant was, she never got flustered."

"But was she telling us the truth, the whole truth and nothing but the truth?" Floyd asked in a facetious tone.

"What do you think?"

"I don't remember catching her out in any fibs."

"But practically everything she told us was what the accused had told her. *She* may have been telling the truth, but was he when he told her all that?"

"You've a point there! Quite frankly, I was so busy looking at her, I didn't always listen to what she was saying." In an attempt to justify himself he added, "It's the judge's summing-up at the end that really counts. One thing for sure, you can write off in advance the speeches made by counsel."

"I want to listen to everything and make up my own mind," Martin said firmly.

"There's youthful idealism! But I admire you for

it, Martin, I honestly do. Alas, I haven't a drop of the stuff left. All drained away by the time I was twenty-one." He paused as he negotiated a right turn. "But don't get a wrong impression of me! I'll play my part when it comes to decision time. Nobody rides rough-shod over Peter Floyd. It's just the slowness of it all that gets on my wick. I keep on thinking of all the deals I'm losing out on."

"I liked the way you stood up to Mr. Hislop when we were discussing the case at lunchtime," Martin said, admiringly.

"He's so self-important that one can't resist stick-ing an occasional pin into him. I'd have been a far better foreman than him. For all his talk, he hasn't a clue how to handle people."

"He was headmaster of my school," Martin said, wryly.

"You're kidding!"

"No, I'm not. He retired the year before I left."

"I haven't seen him greeting you as a long lost pupil."

"That's because he hasn't recognised me. It was a vast school and he never actually taught me."

"Are you going to tell him you were there?"

"I'm saving it up for the right moment."

"Bully for you! Spring it on him next time he tries to put you down!"

They chuckled at the picture thus conjured up.

"You know Joyce Stanley, the woman who smiles all the time and never says anything?" Martin said suddenly.

"I think she's walked out of a nuthouse," Floyd said.

"I believe she's got new dentures and she's afraid they'll drop out if she opens her mouth too far."

"That's nothing to smile about."

"She has to smile all the time because she can't shut her mouth properly. I have an aunt who once had the same problem."

"You've got everything worked out, haven't you?" Floyd remarked genially.

"Unlike you, I find it all fascinating. I wish it didn't have to come to an end. It's much better than sitting in front of a drawing board."

"Can't say I share your enthusiasm. I keep looking at Wimble and thinking, there but for the grace of God go I. Except, of course, he's a millionaire and I have difficulty keeping up my mortgage payments."

"You don't seriously think that, do you? There but for the grace of God go you."

"It's not a bad thing to remind oneself of the thinness of the line that divides murderers from non-murderers."

"I've never had the urge to murder anyone," Martin said robustly.

"Wait till you're married!" He drew up sharply at the kerb. "Here's where you wanted to get out, Martin. See you in the morning back in our classroom."

Martin gave him a small wave as the car shot away again.

His trouble is he can't resist trying to sound outrageous and shock people, but I still like him. Thus ran Martin's thoughts as he walked the hundred yards to his home.

When Isabelle Gentry returned to the judge's lodgings, the butler informed her that a Mrs. Harrington had telephoned and requested that the judge should call her back at her convenience.

Felicity Harrington was the mother of Peter's wife, Fran. She and her husband, who was a surgeon, lived in a large flat near the B.B.C. in Portland Place.

They had four sons and Fran was their only daughter. Felicity had herself qualified as a doctor and still held a part-time appointment.

Isabelle Gentry liked her (not least because she was so obviously fond of her son-in-law) and always enjoyed her company on the occasions they met, though without wishing to make them more frequent.

As she walked down the long corridor of the lodgings toward the secluded niche where the telephone was located, she had no doubt why her son's mother-in-law had called. It was merely a question of the nature of her tidings. Would they be good or bad, or, most likely of all, inconclusive?

"I thought it might be you, Isabelle," Felicity Harrington exclaimed as soon as she heard the voice. "I hope you didn't mind me calling you at your official lodgings. Incidentally, I'm following your case with great interest. We must discuss the medical aspects sometime. But I'm ringing about Peter and Fran. I take it you've heard?"

"I spoke to Peter on the phone yesterday evening and he told me Fran had left him."

"She's here. She's spent most of the day walking around like a tormented soul, which I personally regard as a good sign. The more she agonises over what she's done, the sooner she's likely to return to Peter and her children. Incidentally, I've sent her out to take the dog for a walk, so we can talk freely."

"I gather there's another man. A neighbour who's a widower."

Felicity Harrington snorted. "She's persuaded herself she's in love with him."

"I don't even know his name."

"Patrick Starkey. Gather he's lived all his life in Kenya but returned to this country when his wife

116

became ill and decided to stay on after she died. More's the pity!"

"Does he want to marry Fran if he gets the chance?"

"Heaven knows! I don't think she's too sure about that. But I can imagine that, with two small children, he's looking around for another wife. It seems to be one of these messy situations into which they've allowed themselves to drift. It's the greatest pity that Peter didn't spot it in time and tell the man to keep his eyes elsewhere."

"So what's your prognosis?" Isabelle Gentry enquired.

"I'm hopeful that Fran'll come to her senses. I think she's already missing the children tremendously and I know she's still fond of Peter. It could be that he's taken her a bit for granted of late. Husbands tend to once their marriages have settled into a routine. Women remain romantic for much longer. Don't you agree, Isabelle? You must have come across it all the time when you sat as a divorce judge."

"As a generalisation, it's probably true."

"Anyway, I'm certainly doing my best to bring Fran to her senses, though I can't be as blunt as I would like. That would simply be counter-productive. But my real purpose in calling you was to say all is not lost."

"That, at least, is reassuring news."

"I told Fran that if her grandmother were still alive, she'd not have minced her words. I'm not going to get on to the subject of the young of today, because, on the whole, I thoroughly approve of them, but I do often wish they had a bit more staying power. The trouble is that we live in a world of increasing distraction."

Isabelle Gentry realised she was in danger of listening to a monologue, so said firmly, "Peter's proposing to come up to town on Sunday to see Fran. I'm spending the weekend there, so I'll be able to look after the children."

"I think that's a splendid idea. By Sunday her defences should be crumbling, if they haven't already crumbled."

On this optimistic note Isabelle Gentry rang off, feeling more cheerful than she had all day. She would now go and do her homework on the Wimble case. Her instinct told her that Frank Wimble had almost certainly murdered his wife. The question was, would the prosecution be able to prove it? As to that, her mind remained open.

Graham Tapling had few illusions about his client. He had never cared for him, but then a solicitor isn't required to like his clients. As far as he was concerned, clients as wealthy as Frank Wimble got the service they paid for and part of this service involved a visit to the cells as soon as the court rose and before Wimble was taken back to prison for the night.

Conversation tended to be constrained on such an occasion, but at least Tapling did his best.

"I thought Maureen came through as a first class witness," he said cheerfully. "I'm sure she made an excellent impression on the jury. I was watching them and could tell."

"Why can't I see her?"

"I've explained that, Frank. She's been called as a prosecution witness and no way will she be allowed to see you until the trial's over."

"I still resent the fact that the prosecution was able to force her to give evidence on their side. They couldn't have called her at all if she'd been my wife, you say."

Tapling nodded. "In those circumstances, she wouldn't have been competent to give evidence for the prosecution. As it is, however, I think we've had the best of both worlds as Mr. Coe was presented with a thoroughly cooperative witness for cross-examination. We've done very well by her evidence." He shot his client a quick glance. "It won't be long before you're called. Probably tomorrow afternoon."

"I hope Coe knows what questions to ask me."

"Of course he does. He has a very full proof of your evidence and both Stephen Kitter and myself will be ready to remind him of any point he overlooks."

Frank Wimble was thoughtful for a moment. "What really gets me down is not knowing what's going on inside the jury's heads. How would you like to have your fate decided by twelve complete strangers? Sometimes I want to stand up and shout at them just to get a reaction."

"That wouldn't do you any good, so for heaven's sake don't!"

"And I know that woman with all the beads is dead against me. I can tell from her expression."

"People's expressions are frequently misleading. And, in any event, hers is only one voice out of twelve."

"She's not the only one who thinks I'm guilty."

"Stop being morbid and listen to me. When you go into the box, it's very important that you should appear quietly confident. You mustn't lose your cool or harangue the court. And don't try and score points off counsel! But, above all, show respect for the jury. Remember they'll not only be hanging on

119

every word you utter, but they'll be assessing your demeanour."

"I know, I know. Somehow I've got to persuade those twelve cardboard cut-outs that I'm innocent."

Not for the first time, Graham Tapling reflected that self-made millionaires were not the easiest of clients.

"O.K.," he said, "but still try and remember what I've just said."

It was with a sense of relief that he heard the approach of a prison officer coming to fetch Wimble.

As he followed his client out of the cell, it occurred to him that Frank Wimble had shown one rare virtue. Namely, he wasn't constantly asking his legal advisers to proclaim their belief in his innocence and to embrace everything he told them as the untarnished truth.

Tapling accepted that most clients served up a subtle blend of truth and falsehood. In his experience, it was often a subconscious process that went on in the minds of clients, though he reckoned it would have been carefully calculated in Wimble's case. None of this bothered him. His sole preoccupation was that Coe should successfully guide their client across the thinner ice of his defence and bring him safely to acquittal on the other side.

The fact that Wimble probably had murdered his wife was not his solicitor's concern.

12

Detective Superintendent Barty never had any fears about giving evidence. Over the years he had faced more counsel across court-rooms than he'd had hot dinners and few of them had been able to get more out of him than he was prepared to give. With his iron grey hair and slightly bucolic complexion, he resembled a tough old farmer more than a senior detective officer.

Alan Coe had come across him on a number of occasions and regarded him as stubborn and obdurate.

"You tried very hard, did you not, to obtain a confession from the accused?" Coe said aggressively, when he rose to cross-examine.

"Certainly not."

"Do you mean you didn't try?"

"I interviewed the accused on four separate occasions in the course of my enquiries and put various matters to him. There was no question of trying to get any admissions out of him. I may add that his solicitor was present on each occasion."

"Are you perhaps suggesting that, but for Mr. Tapling's presence, you might have had a more fruitful interview from your point of view?"

The witness shrugged off the taunt. "I'm not making any sort of suggestion," he said stonily.

"After Mrs. Wimble's hand was discovered, is it right to say that you literally left no stone unturned in your efforts to find the rest of her body?"

"We made a number of very thorough and intensive searches."

"In so far as they related to Downview Lodge was the accused perfectly cooperative?"

"He didn't assist us in our searches, if that's what you mean."

"Did you invite him to do so?"

"No."

"I think you know quite well what I meant, officer. Did he make any attempts to frustrate you?"

"No." Then after a well-timed pause, he added, "He wasn't given the opportunity."

"Did you ever make any efforts to trace Mrs. Wimble?"

"Yes. That is, before her hand was found and we presumed her to be dead."

"You must, nevertheless, feel considerably baffled."

"There's nothing new about that."

"You have no doubt in your own mind, have you, that the accused murdered his wife?"

"That's for the jury to say."

Counsel and witness faced each other like two wrestlers in the ring looking for an opening.

"Were you not from the outset convinced that she was dead?"

"It was a possibility that arose at a fairly early stage."

"Before her hand was discovered?"

"Yes."

"When, then?"

"Once all efforts to trace her had failed."

"From that moment you were pretty sure she was dead?"

"Yes."

"And equally sure she had been murdered?"

"If she *was* dead, then murder couldn't be ruled out."

"And accordingly you conducted your investigation as a murder hunt?"

"Yes."

"With but a single suspect in mind?"

"There was certainly one more obvious than any others."

"The accused?"

"Yes."

"You mention others," Coe said sardonically. "Were there, in fact, any?"

Superintendent Barty's mouth puckered as though he had bitten into a lemon.

"Not specifically, though one always keeps an open mind in such circumstances."

"Did your open mind allow you to consider that anybody, apart from the accused himself, had murdered Mrs. Wimble?"

Barty knew that defending counsel was again taunting him in the hope that he would say something to dent his image of fair-minded police officer in the eyes of the jury.

"As I've said, if she *had* been murdered, he was the most obvious suspect."

"So you *were* convinced of his guilt at an early stage?"

"I didn't say that."

"Isn't it the plainest inference from what you've said?"

The witness took a deep breath and exhaled slowly. "I don't accept the word 'convinced.'"

"What word would you prefer, Mr. Barty?" the judge broke in.

"All I'm trying to say, my lady, is that the possibility of the accused having killed his wife and disposed of her body was one of several I examined."

"I'm sure nobody can criticise you for that," Mrs. Justice Gentry said pleasantly. "It seems to me to have been a natural line of enquiry."

Coe frowned. He didn't like being interrupted in the course of a cross-examination. All too often it allowed the fish to slip off the hook. Not that he could pretend to have Superintendent Barty on a hook.

"What I'm suggesting, officer, is that from the moment you decided the accused had murdered his wife, you stubbornly closed your mind to any other possibility."

"I don't think I did."

"You don't sound too sure."

"I'm quite certain I didn't. In any event, I was merely the leader of a team. We were discussing different ideas and theories all the time."

Coe gave him a challenging look. "Surely it's closer to the truth to say you were hell-bent on proving a single theory, namely that the accused had murdered his wife?"

"Not so."

"And that you looked only for evidence to support your theory and ignored anything that pointed in another direction?"

"That's quite untrue."

13

"I must say I sleep safer in my bed with thoughts of policemen like that superintendent around," Mrs. Norrington observed as the jury crowded into their room for lunch.

"As long as you don't automatically believe everything he told us," Peter Floyd said.

Mrs. Norrington looked nonplussed. "I just thought he came across as a thoroughly nice, decent person," she said defensively.

"The two things are not compatible. Being a policeman and a nice, decent person," Floyd replied with a faint note of mockery.

"Oh God! Are you one of those people who says we should never believe anything a policeman tells us?" Gwen Hackford called out, giving her beads a nervous tug.

"No. What I said was that they shouldn't be *automatically* believed. There was a time when everyone accepted a policeman's word as gospel, but not any longer. There've been too many instances of their villainy when dealing with suspects and the like."

"I'm sure Superintendent Barty wasn't lying about

anything," Mrs. Norrington said with new-found robustness. "He had as honest a face as I've seen." She felt like adding, much more so than yours, and rather wished she had on hearing what Peter Floyd said next.

"If I may say so, that's being somewhat naive. The truth is that they have so much practice at deceit, they have no problem in assuming an air of simple honesty."

"I confess I never expected to hear such a cynically expressed view," Mr. Hislop now broke in, his tone coldly disdainful. "I trust no one else supports your blanket condemnation of the police. As far as I'm concerned, they're a fine body of men to whom society owes a debt of gratitude."

"If mine was a blanket condemnation, which it was not, yours is even more a blanket approval."

"You definitely did say that being a policeman and being honest were incompatible," Gwen Hackford remarked. She looked round for support. "You mayn't have meant it, but that's what you said."

"What I said," Floyd retorted indignantly, "was that . . ."

"I suggest we all get on with our lunch," Reg Upham said, raising his voice, "before it gets cold."

"It's cold already," Gwen Hackford said tartly.

"It's bloody cold chicken again," Floyd remarked.

Reg Upham gave Martin Capper a broad wink. "At least that's changed the subject," he said.

14

There was an air of expectancy, not least amongst the jury, when the court resumed after lunch. The prosecution had completed its case and the defence was poised to open.

As soon as she took her seat, Mrs. Justice Gentry turned her benign gaze on defending counsel.

"I gather, Mr. Coe, that you are proposing to call witnesses to fact in addition to your client. In those circumstances, do you propose to open your case to the jury?"

Coe rose with the air of a royal personage being graciously pleased to unveil a plaque.

"May it please your ladyship. You must have been wondering, members of the jury, as you sat listening to a procession of prosecution witnesses, what the defence is to this charge of murder.

"My learned friend, Mr. Donlon, has invited you to draw two inferences from the evidence he has called. First that Mrs. Wimble is dead and secondly that the accused murdered and then disposed of her body.

"The defence also invites you to infer that she is

dead, *but* that she died accidentally or as a result of misadventure.

"What we suggest to you is that this overwrought lady, who had taken to going for walks after dark, went out on the evening of Friday, the twenty-eighth of September, last year and met her death in one of two ways. Either she fell down a crevice or the like and was unable to get out or she was taken ill and sought shelter in one of the many caves in the area where she subsequently died of exposure.

"It is even possible, members of the jury, given her unhappy state of mind that she deliberately lay down and waited for death to come to her.

"If that be the case, you may be saying to yourselves, why has her body, apart from her hand, never been found?

"One answer is that nobody started looking for it until at least two and a half months after she had disappeared and, by that time, anything could have happened to it. Remember that Professor Penny told the court that, in his view, all the flesh could have been eaten away in far less time than that.

"If you're still sceptical and wondering why no other trace has ever been found in the light of all the searches made by the police, just think for a moment of the intensive and unsuccessful searches we've all, from time to time, made in our own homes for some missing article. It's there, but we can't find it. And that, members of the jury, is within the confines of our own home. Here, the police were searching many square miles of countryside. Is it, therefore, all that surprising that they were not successful?

"The prosecution's case is built up of inference. All the defence can do is ask you to draw a quite different inference as to the cause of the deceased's death, bearing in mind one additional, crucial point.

Namely the accused's repugnance to violence and his complete revulsion of the sight of blood."

"Mr. Coe," Mrs. Justice Gentry broke in, "is not the purpose of an opening to outline to the jury the nature of the evidence you are going to call? It occurs to me that you are making a closing rather than an opening speech."

Donlon nodded gravely while Alan Coe assumed an expression of puzzled innocence.

"My lady, I was seeking to make it clear to the jury that the defence didn't dispute the facts so much as the inferences to be drawn from them. Surely I'm entitled to open that to the jury?"

"It's a question of degree, Mr. Coe, and the fact is that you have not, as yet, told the jury the nature of the evidence you'll be calling. You weren't obliged to open the case if you didn't wish to, but having decided to do so, I don't think you should wander into the realm of theorising. At any rate, not until you've established a basis for doing so by telling the jury what your witnesses are going to prove."

Coe assumed a sulky expression, taking umbrage at the suggestion that he had been guilty of wandering in his advocacy.

Turning back to the jury, he said, "Members of the jury, I have little more I wish to say to you at this stage. Apart from the accused, whose evidence I don't propose to detail to you, I shall be calling Dr. Young who was Mrs. Wimble's doctor and Mrs. Duckworth who is the accused's married daughter and who will tell you of her mother's erratic moods in the weeks preceding her disappearance."

He turned, with seeming reluctance, to face the judge again. She was aware that she had ruffled his feathers and regarded his display of pique with complete equanimity.

"With your ladyship's indulgence," he said, "I would like to call Dr. Young ahead of my client. He is here and, like all doctors, an extremely busy person, particularly at this time of year. He would certainly appreciate being called as soon as possible and then released."

"Do you have any objection, Mr. Donlon?" the judge enquired.

"No, my lady. I wouldn't wish to oppose the application simply on the grounds of form."

"Very well, Mr. Coe, let Dr. Young be called now."

Dr. Young, who had given evidence a good many times, though mostly in coroners' courts, had an abiding suspicion of the law and those who practised it. He had once been made to look a fool when giving evidence on behalf of a patient charged with drunken driving and had never been able to forget the experience.

One of the results had been that he now refused to attend court unless first served with a witness summons. And when he did appear, he was at pains to put distance between himself and the law's practitioners.

He took the oath briskly and faced defending counsel with an air of frowning impatience.

"Were you Mrs. Wimble's doctor?" Coe asked, after eliciting the witness's personal details.

"In Little Misten, yes."

"Do you mean she had another doctor elsewhere?"

"I understand she saw one in London on a few occasions."

"But you were her regular doctor?"

"As I've said, I was in Little Misten."

"How long had you looked after her?"

130

"Since she and her husband moved into Downview Lodge which was about four years ago."

"What sort of health did she have?"

"Normal."

"How often used you to see her professionally?"

"I can give you a record of her ailments if you wish."

"I don't think you need itemise them, but what sort of ailments were they?"

"I attended her three times for different virus infections, all of which could be loosely termed influenza. Once for a poisoned toe, once for a sprained wrist..."

"Which wrist was it?" Coe broke in with sudden interest.

"Her right wrist. Do you want me to go on?"

"No, I don't think you need, but let me ask you this, when was the last time you saw Mrs. Wimble professionally before her disappearance?"

The witness glanced at the folder he had brought into court.

"I saw her at my surgery on the tenth of September last year. She asked me to renew a prescription I had given her."

"What was it for?"

"She had come to see me in June when she complained of sleeping badly. I examined her, but could find nothing organically wrong and concluded she was undergoing some emotional stress..."

"Did she tell you the reason for her stress? Just answer yes or no."

"Yes."

"Did it concern her marriage? Again, just yes or no."

"It did," the witness said drily.

"I'm not trying to bottle you up, but the rules of

evidence don't permit us to hear details of what Mrs. Wimble said to you or you to her."

And a typically stupid rule it is, the witness reflected scornfully.

"What had you prescribed when you saw her in June?"

"Tranquillisers and a sleeping pill called Sleeptite which has an amobarbital sodium base."

"Is that a barbiturate?"

"Yes."

"Did you see her between June and September?"

"I met her in the street one day and enquired how she was feeling."

"And when she came back to see you for a renewal of the prescription, did you examine her again?"

"No. It wasn't necessary in my view. I naturally asked her questions about her condition, but that was all."

"Did she seem better or worse than when you'd seen her in June?"

"There was little change. People in her condition are in a constant state of ups and downs. All one can try and do is help them through their down periods."

"You didn't feel she was building up to a crisis? Toward a complete nervous breakdown?"

"No."

"With hindsight, do you think she might have been?"

"There was no evidence of that."

"Did you ever regard her as a possible suicide?"

"There was nothing in her medical history to indicate it. But, then, there often are no advance warning signs before somebody suddenly takes his life."

"Are you aware that she used to go for lonely walks after dark?"

"Yes."

"Did she tell you that?"

"No."

"Who did?"

"The gentleman sitting behind you," he said, nodding in Mr. Tapling's direction.

"How do you view that particular item of behaviour?"

"If it was something new, then I would regard it as a further indication of her nervous condition."

"A deteriorating condition?"

"Not necessarily. She may have found that night walks helped her to sleep better. A lot of people do. Walking can be an excellent therapy in more ways than one."

"But if she had never taken such walks previously and suddenly began doing so, would you not regard that as significant?"

"Not of itself," the witness replied with a touch of asperity.

"God, he's a maddening person!" Coe turned and whispered to his instructing solicitor. "Why didn't you warn me what to expect?" Without waiting for an answer, he faced the witness once more, "What do you mean 'not of itself'?" he asked with an edge to his tone.

"I mean that walking at night is not of itself evidence of abnormal behaviour. It seems to me, as I've already said, that she probably found it a useful therapy, which I can understand. If it helped her to sleep better, it was nature's own prescription which is often more satisfactory than a doctor's."

"He's a complete write-off," Coe muttered to his junior as he sat down. "I'd never have called him if I'd known."

"He hasn't said anything to damage our case," Kitter said in an earnest whisper.

"Nor to enhance it," Coe retorted.

Donlon rose to his feet, adjusted his wig and hitched up his gown. He had been observing Coe's increasing frustration and annoyance with private satisfaction.

"As far as you were concerned, Dr. Young, there was nothing very seriously wrong with Mrs. Wimble?"

"Not in my view."

"When a marriage is in difficulties, isn't it quite natural for those concerned to suffer stress?"

"Yes."

"And is it not a fact that a great many people have become reliant on tranquillisers and sleeping pills?"

"Far too many in my view."

"When you saw Mrs. Wimble two weeks before her disappearance, was there anything to suggest that she was close to complete breakdown in health?"

"No."

"Thank you," Donlon said with a complacent air and resumed his seat.

Coe, who had been having a hurried, whispered conversation with Tapling, rose to address the judge.

"I have been asked to make a further application to your ladyship with regard to the calling of my next witness. It appears that Mrs. Duckworth, whose evidence would have followed the accused's, is here now and would find it extremely difficult to return tomorrow. I accept, of course, that her convenience cannot override the court's. Nevertheless, I would once more ask for your ladyship's indulgence to allow me to call her ahead of the accused. Her evidence is quite short and could be concluded this afternoon if she were to be called straightaway."

Mrs. Justice Gentry glanced down at prosecuting counsel over the top of her spectacles.

"What do you say to that, Mr. Donlon?"

"I leave it to your ladyship's discretion. I neither support nor oppose my learned friend's application."

"Mr. Coe, can you give me some idea of why this witness will find it difficult to be here tomorrow?" the judge asked.

Coe turned to receive further whispered words from his solicitor.

"I understand, my lady, that she has promised to accompany her mother-in-law who has an appointment to see a consultant surgeon about a possible serious operation."

The judge looked thoughtful, then turned toward the jury.

"In case you're wondering what this is all about, members of the jury, let me explain. It is established practice that where the defence are proposing to call witnesses to fact in addition to the accused, the accused shall give his evidence first. This obviates any later suggestion that he has trimmed his evidence in the light of what he has heard his witnesses say. It is not, however, an absolute rule and a judge is entitled to exercise his discretion if there be reasonable grounds for so doing. Having heard what Mr. Coe has to say and noting that Mr. Donlon remains neutral, I am of the opinion that no harm will be done if I accede to the application."

"I am most grateful to your ladyship and also to my learned friend," Coe said. He had not expected to be so readily accommodated.

Alison Duckworth came into court and made her way to the witness box. She was wearing a russet red wool coat over a dress which also reflected autumn colours.

She was a handsome, rather than a pretty, woman, being big-boned and strong-featured. Her dark

135

brown hair had a sheen as though she had spent her time outside the court brushing it.

A determined-looking young woman, Mrs. Justice Gentry thought as she watched her take the oath. She had noticed, too, how Brian Wimble had sat forward with an intent expression when his sister came into court.

Alan Coe elicited that the witness was twenty-four years old and lived in South Kensington with her husband who was a stockbroker. She had been married three years, but didn't have any children.

While he was taking her through these preliminaries, she cast her father frequent small smiles of encouragement. He, for his part, observed her with a fondness that had been totally absent when his son had been in the box.

"When was the last time you saw your mother?" Coe now asked.

"A week before she disappeared. I went down to pick up some house linen she was letting me have."

"Was your father there?"

"No, only my mother."

"How did you find her?"

"I thought she seemed distracted and vague. Also rather depressed."

"How did her vagueness manifest itself?"

"She'd start to say something and her voice would drift away and she wouldn't finish the sentence."

"Did you know the cause of her depression?"

"My father had been pressing her for a divorce for some time and I think she was feeling the strain. She could be very obstinate and she just wouldn't face up to the fact that her marriage had broken down."

"Had you seen her earlier that month?"

136

"Yes. I had driven down about ten days earlier to collect some apples and tomatoes from the garden."

"Was that at your mother's suggestion?"

"No, my father's. He told me to go and help myself."

"How was your mother on that occasion?"

"Much the same as the following week."

"Used she to discuss her problems with you?"

"I knew precisely what her problem was. I merely tried to get her to accept the inevitable."

"Were you aware of her habit of going for walks at night?"

"Yes. It struck me as odd, but harmless."

"Do you think she'd have been capable of committing suicide?"

"I don't think you're entitled to elicit the witness's opinion, Mr. Coe," the judge said firmly.

"Let me rephrase my question," Coe said. "Did she ever show any suicidal tendencies?"

"I can't say she did."

"Would she have had any religious or moral scruples about taking her own life?"

"None that I'm aware of. I certainly never heard her voice any."

"Coming to a different topic, Mrs. Duckworth, what was your father's reaction to the sight of blood?"

"He was liable to faint," she said with a small laugh. "He was more than just squeamish."

"And what was his reaction to violence even if it didn't involve the spilling of blood?"

"He couldn't bear to watch it."

"Have you ever known him offer violence to anyone?"

"Never."

"Was he ever violent toward your mother?"

"Never. He sometimes lost his temper and shouted at her—well, at me and my brother, too, if it comes to that—but physical violence never."

Coe gave a satisfied nod and sat down.

The witness wore a guarded expression as prosecuting counsel rose to cross-examine her.

"Have you always been very close to your father?" Donlon asked.

"Yes," she said after a second's hesitation.

"I had the impression from your evidence that you get on better with him than you did with your mother. Is that a fair statement?"

The corners of her mouth turned down as if she was being asked to pick up something disagreeable.

"I've always been very fond of my father," she said, with a note of defiance.

The fact that she so obviously avoided answering his question seemed to satisfy Donlon.

"I also had the impression," he went on, "that you didn't have much sympathy with your mother's attitude toward a divorce. Is that so?"

"I suppose it is. I didn't think she was being wholly reasonable."

"You used the word 'obstinate' when describing her attitude earlier. Do you stand by that?"

"Yes, I do," she said after a moment's pause.

"Are you prepared to do all you can to assist your father?"

"Certainly, I am." She seemed suddenly aware she was stepping on to dangerous ground. "Though everything I've said in this court is the truth."

Donlon made a small deprecating gesture and sat down.

"I have just one or two questions to put in re-examination," Coe said, when the judge glanced enquiringly in his direction.

"You have no need to feel ashamed of supporting your father..."

"I don't," the witness snapped.

"That didn't sound like a question to me, Mr. Coe," the judge also broke in.

"It would have been a question, my lady, but it got intercepted in its prelude."

"If you can put your questions without any preludes, you won't run into the same difficulty again," Mrs. Justice Gentry remarked with a sardonic gleam.

"Let me start again," Coe said good-humouredly. "Has the fact that you're very fond of your father in any way distorted your perspective?"

"No."

"Were you also fond of your mother?"

"Yes, of course I was," the witness said in a tone which was a mixture of impatience and embarrassment.

"And have you given the court a fair and truthful assessment of your mother's condition?"

"Yes."

"Thank you, Mrs. Duckworth, that is all I wish to ask you."

Mrs. Justice Gentry looked up at the clock and decided the court could suitably adjourn for the day. It didn't seem to her that either of Alan Coe's witnesses had done much to advance his case. Certainly neither good nor harm had accrued to either side by her decision to allow them to be called out of sequence. She became aware that defending counsel was still on his feet and wishing to address her.

"Yes, Mr. Coe," she said in an enquiring tone.

"I am instructed, my lady, to ask for your permission for Mrs. Duckworth to visit her father before she returns to London."

The judge shook her head. "No, I don't think that

would be at all proper at this stage, with his evidence still to come."

"I quite understand, my lady," Coe said quickly. "It was only because I was expressly asked to make the application ..."

"Say no more, Mr. Coe. I, too, understand."

A few minutes later, she was on her way back to the lodgings in the ancient and dignified Rolls Royce which the county produced for ferrying its visiting High Court judge to and from court.

She reckoned that most of the next day, Friday, would be taken up with the accused's evidence. That would mean speeches and her summing-up on Monday, with a verdict either that evening or on Tuesday.

More and more it seemed to her to be essentially a case for the jury to decide for itself with minimum judicial influence.

15

Brian Wimble was waiting on the pavement outside when his sister emerged from the court building.

"Oh, hello," she said without enthusiasm when he greeted her. "I saw you sitting there watching me while I was giving my evidence. Are you proposing to stay to the bitter end?"

He nodded. "I feel I have to."

"Why the interest now when you barely troubled to see daddy all the months he was awaiting trial?"

"The trial itself is rather different."

"What do you think is going to happen?" she asked in a brittle tone.

"I've no idea." With a faint smile he added, "Even though I've recently done some psychiatric medicine, I still can't read a jury's mind."

"I suppose you hope he'll be found guilty?"

"It's not exactly something to wish on oneself. A father convicted of murder."

"But wouldn't you rather that than the thought of a guilty man going free?" she said in a hectoring tone. "You were always one for high moral stances."

He passed his tongue over his lips and said with a

curiously lopsided smile, "As a matter of fact, I don't believe he did murder her."

"What do you think did happen then?" she asked sharply.

He shrugged. "Your guess is as good as mine."

She gave him a puzzled look. "Do you know something that I don't, Brian?" she asked in a suspicious voice.

"What could I know?"

"That's what I'd like to find out! But I can't stand here talking. I have to drive back to town." She gave her brother a glance of frowning appraisal. "I can't make you out, Brian. But then I never could."

"I doubt whether you've ever tried," he remarked, with another curious little smile. "Any more than father did."

After a conspiratorial glance about her to ensure she couldn't be overheard, Edith Norrington said, "I didn't care for that young woman who gave evidence this afternoon."

Gwen Hackford, to whom the observation was addressed as they waited for a bus down the road from the court-house, gave a brisk nod.

"Wouldn't be surprised to learn there was an incestuous relationship between them," she remarked.

Mrs. Norrington was visibly shocked. "Oh, I never meant that," she said. "I'm sure there was nothing of that sort."

"I'm only saying it wouldn't surprise me to hear there was. Not that it's likely to come out. But it's much commoner than you'd suppose. Particularly between a strong-willed father and a favourite daughter."

Mrs. Norrington, whose world was a million light years removed from that of incest, felt she must quickly change the subject. She had always imagined that incest was strictly confined to the lower orders. The suggestion that people in the Wimbles' walk of life might practise it stunned her. Murder was one thing, but incest...

"I have a friend at Little Misten who is one of Dr. Young's patients," she said.

"If his evidence was meant to show that Mrs. Wimble was a suicidal neurotic, it was about as effective as a damp match. You could see defending counsel getting quite testy with him."

"I must say, I do like the look of our judge," Mrs. Norrington observed in a further effort to say something unexceptionable.

"I read a profile of her in a magazine a few weeks ago," Gwen replied in an offhand tone, her hands thrust deep into the pockets of her duffel coat, her beads, for once, at rest.

"Did she sound as nice as she looks?"

"She sounded like a cosy grandmother who'd made it to judge," Gwen said with a faint note of scorn.

"One has to admire women who get to the top of the tree."

"Like dogs that can walk on their hind-legs, I suppose."

Edith Norrington sighed. There was certainly nothing cosy about conversation with Gwen Hackford. She turned with relief when a voice behind them suddenly spoke.

"Hello, ladies, are we all waiting for the same bus?" said Reg Upham, who had just joined them.

"What did *you* think of Alison Duckworth?" Gwen asked bluntly.

"Didn't have a lot to say, did she?" Reg replied, scratching the lobe of one ear.

"Mrs. Norrington didn't like her," Gwen went on with the determined air of somebody intent on squeezing dry every lemon within reach.

"I merely said I didn't care for her manner. What I really mean is I'm glad she's not my daughter."

"I couldn't help noticing the way her father looked at her while she was giving evidence," Reg remarked. "Real lustful looks they were at times."

"There!" Gwen said triumphantly. "It bears out what I said to you. I bet he has committed incest with her. Mentally, if not physically."

"I'm afraid I'm only an ordinary housewife," Mrs. Norrington said stiffly. "I don't occupy my mind with such thoughts."

Gwen gave a throaty laugh. "But you're not an ordinary housewife this week, you're a Crown Court juror trying a murder case."

It was with considerable relief that Edith Norrington saw the approach of her bus. At least she'd soon be back in her familiar kitchen immersed in preparing her family's dinner.

It seemed to Jean Hislop that her husband returned from court looking more put out and annoyed each day.

"Go and sit down, dear and I'll bring you a cup of tea," she said, giving him her customary greeting as she helped him off with his top coat and took his hat.

"I could certainly do with one," he remarked with a heavy sigh.

"How's it gone today?" she asked, on returning with his tea and a single chocolate biscuit in the saucer.

"I'm going to have all my work cut out guiding that lot through a reasoned discussion," he said with a small bitter laugh.

"I'm sure they'll listen to you when the time comes, dear."

"It's all I can do to prevent anarchy taking over. One or two of them are plainly anti-authority and downright ill-mannered. What with controlling them and trying to stir something out of others who are no more than sheep, it's an uphill task."

"I'm sure you're equal to it."

"I like to think so, but there are moments when I begin to wonder. I shouldn't be talking like this, but there's one terrible man whose only thought is to get back to his money-grubbing job. He's completely un-suited to sit on a jury. Then there's a youth who can't be more than nineteen and who clearly thinks he knows everything. Unfortunately, he takes his lead from this other dreadful fellow. And there's a woman who's not much help either. She has 'militant femi-nist' written all over her." He shook his head de-spairingly. "Chairing a staff meeting was child's play compared with being foreman of this jury."

His wife gave him an indulgent smile. "You'll find a way to deal with them. I've never known you fail yet in anything you undertook."

Ralph Hislop accepted the accolade with a nod. "You remember my mentioning a woman who smiles but never speaks? I tried to draw her out at lunch-time today, but didn't have much success. There's something very odd about her. She gave me a most curious look when I said I supposed she'd never been inside a court before."

"Why was that?"

"Why was what?" he asked testily.

"I don't follow why she gave you a curious look."

"No more do I. You can't have been listening to what I said. She's completely useless as a juror, of course." He sighed. "It really isn't a very satisfactory

145

system that allows so many unsuitable people to be summoned for jury service. They need to apply some sort of intelligence test to weed out all the riff-raff."

"Who did you have giving evidence today?" Her tone was the same as if she were asking who had topped the bill in a variety show.

"There was a detective superintendent, who seemed a very sound chap. Then there was a doctor and the daughter of the accused."

"Oh, that must have been interesting. What was she like?"

"You know I'm not allowed to discuss the case," he said severely.

"Would you like another cup of tea, then?" she enquired.

He held his cup out for her to take and she departed to the kitchen. Thirty-five years of marriage to an authoritarian figure had drained away any self-assertion. Even as the wife of the headmaster of a large school she had remained in the background of his professional life. It was where he had placed her when they first became married and where she had dwelt ever since.

As she poured him out another cup of tea, she found herself thinking about his troublesome fellow jurors and couldn't help smiling.

16

The appearance in the witness box of someone charged with murder is always the star attraction of the trial and this was borne out the next morning when the court resumed. The press, whose interest had begun to flag toward the end of the prosecution's case, was back in full force.

As Frank Wimble made his way from the dock to the witness box, a hundred pair of eyes watched him with a mixture of emotions.

This was the moment at which he stood on display. His hair shone in the light beamed down on the witness box and the way it curled thickly in the nape of his neck seemed to give him an aura of virility. He was dressed in the same dark business suit he had worn throughout the trial, but had on a fresh shirt and tie. The shirt had broad stripes of white and crushed strawberry and the tie was royal blue. He was not only a well-groomed figure, but an utterly confident-looking one as well.

His answers to Alan Coe's preliminary questions came with calm assurance. He gave his full name and address, his age (fifty), the length of time he had been married (twenty-seven years), the names of his children (Brian and Alison) and a brief history of the build-up of his business (wholesale men's clothing) which he had sold four years before for three million pounds. Finally he referred to his latest business enterprise, a small electronics company in which he held a major stake.

"At the time you sold your men's clothing business, did you intend to start up in another field?" Coe asked.

"Quite the reverse. I intended to retire and take life easy. After all, I'd made enough money to do that."

"What caused you to change your mind?"

Wimble gave a rueful shrug. "Boredom. Plain boredom. I'd worked hard all my life building up my business and I became restless doing nothing."

"Have you always been a very active person?"

"Always. I'm what they call a workaholic. My new business was on the way to making me another fortune before all this happened."

"I want to ask you some questions about your marriage. Was it a happy one?"

"I always thought so. It had its bumpy patches, of course, but what marriage doesn't? My wife never wanted for anything."

Except possibly love and companionship, Mrs. Justice Gentry thought to herself.

"When did things start to go wrong?"

"I've had time to think about that in recent months," he said grimly. "I think we had been slowly drifting apart for some time. The turning point probably came when the children grew up and left home."

"There wasn't any sudden change in your wife's attitude?"

"No. Elspeth had always been a fairly reserved person. She was adept at hiding her feelings when she wished to."

"And about two and a half years ago you met Mrs. Yates?"

"Yes."

"And shortly thereafter did she become your mistress?"

"Yes."

"When did you first raise the question of divorce with your wife?"

"In the early part of last year."

"That is, about eight or nine months before her disappearance?"

"Near enough."

"What was her reaction?"

"She flatly refused to consider it."

"So what did you do?"

Frank Wimble gave a slightly tigerish smile. "Raised it again and went on raising it. I've learnt in business that one rarely gets what one wants at the first asking and that persistence is the name of the game."

He appeared rather pleased with his answer and was quite unaware of its chilly reception by the judge whose expression revealed not a flicker as she underlined the note she had made.

"And did your wife continue to refuse you a divorce?"

"I'm afraid she did."

"Did you ever row with her about it?"

"You mean the time Brian referred to in his evidence?"

"All right, let's deal with that occasion first. What happened?"

"I raised the subject again and she flatly refused to discuss it."

"Did you shout abuse at her?"

"Certainly not. I may have slammed the door as I left the room, but that was all. I'm afraid Brian has always tended to exaggerate. He was very much on his mother's side over this, as on all other occasions, and it coloured his judgment."

"And were there other similar occasions? Occasions, that is, when you became annoyed by her attitude?"

"I can't deny it," he said, as though owning up to a distant act of petty pilfering. "I'm afraid it usually ended up with me raising my voice. I felt she was being unreasonable and it used to annoy me that she wouldn't even discuss the subject."

"Did you ever offer her violence?"

"Never. The very thought of violence nauseates me."

"And what's your reaction to the sight of blood?"

"It's true what the witnesses have said. I come over faint. I've been like it all my life. You can ask anyone."

"Had you observed any change in your wife's health during the few weeks before her disappearance?"

"I'm afraid I was too preoccupied with my own affairs to notice anything. I knew she'd begun to go for evening walks."

"Did she tell you?"

"No, my daughter, Alison, did."

"How often were you seeing her at that time?"

"I was spending the best part of each week in London, but I'd get away to Downview Lodge about every other weekend."

"What were you proposing to do in the light of your wife's refusal to give you a divorce?"

"There was nothing I could do except wait for five years until I could apply for one myself on whatever the grounds are."

"And were you prepared to wait?"

"I had no choice."

"Did it ever enter your head to murder your wife?"

"Never. Never. I couldn't murder anyone for the reasons I've stated." As he spoke he turned his head and gave the jury a quick, appraising glance. Several of them looked uncomfortably away, but a number of others, including Martin and Gwen Hackford, stared calmly back at him.

Coe turned a page of his brief with the air of opening a new chapter.

"Let me now come to Friday, September the twenty-eighth last year. Where were you that day?"

"In London until the evening. I had a long meeting in the morning, followed by a business lunch and a further meeting in the afternoon that ran beyond its scheduled time. The result was that I didn't get away until around eight o'clock when I drove down to Little Misten."

"What time did you arrive there?"

"I had a number of hold-ups on the way and didn't get there until just before nine thirty."

"And what did you discover when you reached home?"

"The house was empty."

"Were you expecting to find your wife there?"

"Yes."

"When had you last seen her?"

"The previous weekend. But I had spoken to her

on the phone the night before and told her to expect me in time for a late dinner the next evening."

"How had she seemed when you talked to her on the phone on Thursday evening?"

"Perfectly normal. Though, looking back, I was aware of a certain reticence in her manner, not that I thought anything of it at the time."

"At all events, there was nothing in her manner to alarm you?"

"Absolutely not."

"You say that the house was empty on your arrival. Were any of the lights on?"

"Yes. Most of those downstairs."

"Tell us what happened next."

"I parked my car in the garage beside hers and let myself into the house..."

"Was the door locked or unlocked?"

"Locked."

"Was that usual?"

"Yes. When she was alone in the house, she always locked the front and back doors after dark."

"Yes, go on."

"I put my briefcase down on the hall table and called out her name. When I got no reply, I poked my head into various downstairs rooms. Then I went upstairs as I thought she might have gone to lie down and dropped off to sleep. But there was no sign of her anywhere."

"What did you do then?"

"I got myself a drink and went and sat down. I assumed she had gone out and would soon be back."

"Where did you think she might have gone?"

"Either for one of her evening walks or possibly to visit somebody. I looked to see if she had left me a note, but she hadn't."

"Yes, what next?"

"I must have fallen asleep in my chair. It was after midnight when I woke up. It was obvious she still hadn't returned and I began to be worried. First of all, I went and searched the outbuildings and garden, thinking she may have collapsed outside. Then around one o'clock, by which time I was really worried, I set off in my car with the idea of searching some of the nearby lanes. I realised almost immediately that it was a hopeless task."

"Were you aware of a car behind you as you turned out of Downview Lodge?"

"I really can't recall."

"Dr. Farrer says that your car quickly accelerated away from his. Would you accept that?"

"It's a fast car," the witness said with a shrug. "Also I was in something of a panic. I'd set off an on impulse and, as I've said, almost immediately realised what a hopeless task I'd given myself."

"How long were you out?"

"Not more than fifteen minutes."

"What did you do when you got home?"

"I had another drink and went upstairs to bed."

"My learned friend will certainly ask you if I don't; but did it occur to you to telephone the police or any of her friends?"

"It was too late to start calling her friends and, in any event, if something had happened to her while she was with them, they'd have been through to me. As for the police, it seemed premature to alert them."

"Do you know what she'd have been wearing when she disappeared?"

"Only by working it out later and trying to assess what was missing. I think it must have been a bluey grey dress, the shoes she always kept downstairs for going out in and a speckled brown coat. I couldn't find any of them later, but I don't pretend to remember every dress she had and she may have been wearing something quite different."

"Apart from what she was wearing, did she take anything else with her?"

"Not as far as I could tell."

"What about money?"

"There was always four or five hundred pounds in cash in the house. Sometimes over a thousand. I can't tell you whether she took any."

"Did you find any left?"

"There was about three hundred."

"Does that indicate that she probably did take some?"

"It points that way."

"What happened the next morning?"

"I was up early, soon after six. There was still no sign of her. I made a further search of the garden and outbuildings when it was light. Then I came in, had some coffee and sat down to try and think straight."

"By then, had you come to a different conclusion as to what might have happened to her?"

"Yes, I was beginning to think she had literally walked out on me."

"What brought you to that view?"

"I'd had a lot of time to think during the night and suddenly various bits seemed to fall into place. Her increasing air of detachment and her secretive silences when we were together made me wonder whether she'd not had a boyfriend hidden away somewhere and might have left me for him. It would have been typical of her to choose her moment and do it that way in order, she would feel, to teach me a lesson for my behaviour." The witness turned and gave the jury a rueful glance. "And, of course, this

154

was confirmed when she phoned me three days later and said she had left me for good and I'd never see her again."

"Coming back to that Saturday morning, why did you tell Mrs. Passingham that your wife had gone to visit a sick aunt?"

"I didn't want her to ask a lot of questions and I was embarrassed to tell her what I then believed had happened." He made a slight grimace. "I hardly wanted to blurt out to our cleaning woman that my wife had packed up and left me for another man. Particularly as I've always been aware that Mrs. Passingham didn't like me."

"Were you at Downview Lodge when you received this call from your wife three days later?"

"Yes. I spent the whole of the following week there. I felt I had to stay around until I knew for certain what had happened."

"In the middle of December, you received a visit from Police Constable Jameson?"

"Yes, on a Saturday morning. He asked me where my wife was and I told him immediately she had left me and that I had no idea where she'd gone. He later asked me if I was aware of the rumours circulating in the village and I told him that I was as I'd received an anonymous telephone call."

"Come January, did you receive further visits from the police?"

"I lost count of how many."

"And did they make thorough searches of the house and garden?"

"Several times."

"Always with your consent and cooperation?"

"Absolutely. In fact, I welcomed their action as I had nothing to hide and was only anxious to be cleared of all suspicion. My life had rapidly become a nightmare and there seemed to be nothing I could do."

"As we now know, your wife's fleshless hand came to light on the twenty-third of March when it was found by a dog about eight miles from Little Misten. When were you first told of its discovery?"

"I think it was the next day that the police got in touch with me."

"What was your reaction when they told you?"

"I was completely stunned. I couldn't believe it."

"It means, of course, that your wife must have returned to the district after she had spoken to you on the telephone. Can you think of any reason why she should have done that?"

"None. I've even wondered whether she ever left the district. It's possible that she was hiding at a friend's house." He gave the jury a helpless look. "But if she did go away and come back, I'm at a complete loss to explain it. I've thought and thought about it without reaching an answer."

"That she is dead can't be disputed," Coe said gravely, "but did you play any part in causing her death?"

"So help me God, I never did."

Mrs. Justice Gentry always mistrusted witnesses who unnecessarily invoked the deity. And when the witness also happened to be the accused, she was doubly mistrustful. None of this showed on her face, however, as she signalled prosecuting counsel to begin his cross-examination.

Donlon gave his gown a hitch and the witness a long, hard stare.

Leaning forward over his small portable lectern, he said, "You have changed your story whenever circumstances required it, have you not?"

"Certainly not."

156

"You first said that your wife had gone to visit a sick aunt. Was that true or was it a lie?"

"It was not true, but I've explained . . ."

"So it was a lie?"

The witness gave a disdainful shrug.

"I immediately admitted it to P.C. Jameson."

"And told him that she had gone off with another man to you knew not where. Was that true or was it a lie?"

"I believed it to be true at the time."

"Or did you believe that her body would never be found and that you could safely get away with that story?"

"I can only repeat what I said just now. I believed it to be true at the time."

"You really believed that she had run off with a man of whose existence, let alone identity, you had not the slightest idea? Is that what you are asking the jury to believe?"

"Yes, I am."

"And then after her hand has been found, you change your story once again and are now inviting the jury to infer that your wife had an accident or committed suicide. Is that your final position?"

Alan Coe jumped to his feet. "My learned friend is being most unfair. The witness has never in the course of his evidence suggested to the jury what inferences should be drawn from the finding of the hand."

"Well, what is your final position?" Donlon asked, unabashed.

In the circumstances, Mrs. Justice Gentry decided not to blow her referee's whistle but to let play continue.

Wimble said, "All I'm saying—all I can say—is

that I had nothing to do with my wife's death, however it came about."

"Is it not a fact that it has nevertheless cleared your way to marry Mrs. Yates?"

"Yes, but that was not my doing."

"Would you agree that you had a vested interest in her death?"

"Not put like that."

"But it's true, isn't it?"

"I certainly didn't want her dead sufficiently to kill her."

"How much did you want her dead then?"

"Not at all," the witness snapped, in an effort to retrieve his previous answer.

"But her death came at a convenient moment for you?"

"I never believed she was dead until her hand was found."

"By suggesting to the police that she had run away with another man, were you not hoping to get them off your tail?"

"If that ever had been my hope, which it hadn't, I was singularly unsuccessful," Wimble said in a sarcastic voice.

"I want to ask you about this revulsion toward violence and the sight of blood that you profess to have. Is it really as bad as you've made out?"

"My son and daughter have testified to it."

"I know that. Do you regard yourself as a tough business man?"

"You have to be tough to get where I am."

"And ruthless, too?"

"You have to be prepared to be ruthless if necessary."

"To trample on anyone who stands in your path?"

"Yes, but not in a physical sense."

"Did you ever have any qualms about beating down your competitors?"

"None. But I never physically knocked them down. I couldn't have done that."

"Given the necessary circumstances, would you be prepared to employ others to do your dirty work for you? By dirty work I mean the use of physical force to achieve your ends?"

"Not if it meant breaking the law," the witness replied after a second's hesitation.

Pray God he doesn't glance around for applause, thought his counsel. To his relief, Frank Wimble resisted the temptation.

"You said in answer to my learned friend that you couldn't ever murder anybody because of your excessive squeamishness about violence and bloodshed. Would that be all that would deter you?"

Wimble frowned angrily. "You're twisting what I said."

Donlon shook his head. "I have a note of it. 'I couldn't murder anyone for the reasons I've stated' were your precise words. I repeat my question. Would that be all that would deter you?"

The witness gave prosecuting counsel a furious glare. "I've never wanted to murder anyone and I never have."

"Of course," Donlon went on in the same conversational tone, "if you wanted to murder somebody without using violence or spilling blood, poison would be the most effective way. Do you agree?"

Wimble once more gripped the ledge of the witness box, though not before a number of jurors had noticed a sudden trembling of his hands.

"I've never tried to poison anyone," he said in a tight voice.

"But you agree that it would involve neither violence nor the spilling of blood?"

"I've never thought about it."

"Think about it now and give me an answer."

"All right, I suppose it wouldn't," he said with a shrug.

"When you arrived home that Friday evening and found the house empty, you've told the court that you assumed your wife had either gone out for one of her walks or to visit a friend. Didn't either course strike you as very curious?"

"No."

"But you had told her to expect you for a late dinner, had you not?"

"Yes."

"Instead of which she had gone out without so much as a note of explanation?"

"Yes."

"Nor, I gather, was there any dinner waiting in the oven?"

"Correct."

"Was the table laid?"

"I can't remember."

"Presumably you looked?"

"If I did, I don't remember."

"But weren't you worried as to what had happened to her? Lights on, but no meal prepared."

"As I've explained, my wife had been behaving rather oddly and I attributed everything to that."

"So you got yourself a drink, sat down and fell asleep?"

"Yes."

"And when you woke up around one o'clock in the morning, you made a further search and then set out in your car to look for her?"

"Yes."

"In something of a panic, you said in answer to my learned friend's question?"

"Yes."

"Why were you in a panic?"

"Because by then I was getting very worried about her."

"Nevertheless fifteen minutes later you returned home, gave yourself another drink and went up to bed?"

"Yes."

"Are we to assume that your panic had evaporated by then?"

"No. Merely that I had it under control."

"What I'm unable to understand is that one moment you're out searching the darkened countryside in a panic and the next you're going off to bed with a drink, without having made the smallest attempt to ring any of your neighbours or invoke the help of the police. Would you like to explain such an apparent inconsistency in your conduct?"

Small beads of perspiration glistened on the witness's upper lip.

"I thought I had," he said with a slight crack in his voice. "In the first place I didn't wish to disturb the neighbours at that late hour. In the second, I decided to leave it until the morning before getting in touch with the police."

"Are you saying that your neighbours' convenience took precedence over your wife's well-being?"

"You know damn well I don't mean that," he shouted. Then turning quickly to the judge, he said in a calmer voice, "I apologise for my outburst."

"You don't do yourself any service by getting angry with counsel," Mrs. Justice Gentry observed.

"But you still didn't get in touch with the police the next morning, did you?"

"I've already explained. By then I'd come to to the conclusion that my wife had walked out on me."

"I want to ask you some questions about that. Would you agree that it was a most remarkable conclusion to reach?"

"No, I wouldn't. If I'd not been so preoccupied with my own affairs, I would have realised it sooner."

"But why should she have refused to divorce you, if she had a lover of her own in the background?"

"To get her own back on me, of course."

"Wouldn't you have expected her to give you your freedom in order to obtain her own?"

"Not necessarily. You didn't know Elspeth. It was in keeping with her character to refuse me a divorce in order to thwart me."

"And then to walk out on you without warning?"

"Yes. She wanted to pay me back for what she thought I'd done to her."

"And yet she phoned you three days later?"

"Yes."

"That was hardly consistent with the attitude you've just described, was it?"

"She must have had some reason of her own for doing so."

"Such as?"

"I can't explain."

"Or have you invented that telephone call?"

"Certainly not."

"Invented it in an effort to prevent the police suspecting you of murder?"

"It certainly didn't achieve that," the witness said bitterly.

"Nevertheless, wasn't that your hope?"

"No."

"Don't you agree that if, as you say you believed, your wife had suddenly deserted you, it's quite extraordinary that she left behind every possession save what she was wearing? Would you not have expected her to take, at least, her jewelry and some clothes?"

"Again you have to have known Elspeth to understand. She was determined to make a complete break with her former existence and start a fresh life without any reminders of the past."

"In that event, why on earth should she have taken the trouble to telephone you?"

"I can only say that she was behaving rather oddly at the time."

"Is that all you can say?"

"Yes. She just wasn't behaving in a rational manner."

Donlon gave his gown a vigorous hoist. "I have to put it to you that her supposed phone call is a complete invention on your part? Moreover that at the time it was allegedly made, your wife had already died by your hand?"

"Quite untrue."

"If she had really walked out on you and had really called you to say so, what on earth could have brought her back to the district?"

"I've already said I can't explain that. Unless she had never left the area."

"But that's even more remarkable, isn't it? It presupposes that she spent three days hiding somewhere locally, then phoned you to say you'll never see her again. Are you really asking the jury to believe that?"

"I've said I can't explain it," Wimble said sharply.

"You can't explain it, I suggest, because like so much of your evidence it's facile improvisation on your part?"

"That's not true."

"For three days after her disappearance and before receiving the supposed phone call, you remained at Downview Lodge. Am I right?"

"Yes."

"And during that period, you made no attempt to notify the police?"

"I'd decided I would wait a week before doing so."

"Why?"

"Because I might hear from her."

"As, if you're to be believed, you did. Her phone call, indicating that she was still alive, absolved you from the need to report her disappearance to the police, did it not?"

"Yes."

"Is that why you invented it?"

"I did not invent it," the witness said in a raised voice, which brought him a sharp glance from the judge.

In Mrs. Justice Gentry's view, few cross-examiners knew when to sit down. There was always the temptation to go on, often with the result that earlier well-scored points became forgotten and the witness was given the opportunity of rehabilitating himself. This was particularly so in the case of an accused.

By the time that Donlon eventually sat down, she felt that he and the witness were locked in a stalemate and that prosecuting counsel's earlier more telling thrusts had lost their impact.

It was, moreover, apparent to her that the jury's attention had begun to wander, a sure sign that counsel was outstaying his welcome.

Realising, however, that he was nearing the end she had been loth to interrupt him, with the result that it was almost one thirty when the court adjourned for lunch. For the past twenty minutes, she

164

had been studiously ignoring a succession of ostentatious glances at watches and the court-room clock.

"We'll resume at two thirty," she announced, giving the jury a friendly beam.

17

"I began to think the old girl wasn't going to let us have any lunch today," Peter Floyd remarked to Martin as they trooped along the corridor to their retiring room. "Mind you, if it's bloody cold chicken again, they can stuff it." He paused on the threshold and stared at the plates of food laid out on the table. "A slice of pie, tastefully garnished with a flabby lettuce leaf and two bits of plastic tomato."

"You haven't come here for the cuisine," Gwen observed, tartly.

"Now she tells me!"

"I enjoyed this morning," Martin said, glancing keenly round the table to see on which plate the largest portion of pie was located and then steering his way toward it.

"If only those two counsel could inject a bit of urgency into the proceedings. Anyone would think they get paid by the hour the way they spin things out."

"In a sense, they do," Gwen said. "They get a brief fee and then what are called refreshers for each day after the first. I happen to know because my father was a barrister."

By this time everyone was seated, with Mr. Hislop in his usual place from where he hoped to be able to control discussion.

"What did you think of him?" Martin said conversationally to Mrs. Norrington who was sitting next to him.

She was in the process of examining the underside of her lettuce leaf and started when he spoke.

"I'm so sorry," she said distractedly. "What did I think of whom?"

"Of Wimble. I must say I wouldn't want to stand in that box and face cross-examination. And I've not even committed a murder."

Mr. Hislop cleared his throat noisily to claim attention. "I really do think we ought to be careful about airing our views at this stage. Prejudging the case is, I suggest, most imprudent," he said, staring pointedly at Martin.

"What do you mean, prejudging the case?" Martin asked indignantly.

"You implied he was guilty," Mr. Hislop said icily.

"I didn't do anything of the sort. Did I, Mrs. Norrington?"

"I certainly didn't take it that way," she said peaceably.

"I still think we should be especially careful what we say at this delicate stage of the trial," Mr. Hislop said with a tight-lipped air.

"I can't see what you've got against healthy, free-ranging discussion," Gwen remarked.

"If it comes to that, nor can I," Peter Floyd chimed in. "Anyway, what would you like us to talk about?"

Two spots of colour appeared on the foreman's

cheeks. In all his years he had never been confronted by such unruliness and been so impotent to handle it.

"I'm only offering you my advice," he said in a constricted voice.

"I'm sure we're glad to have it," Gwen replied, "even if we don't all necessarily agree with it." Casting a challenging glance round the table, she went on, "If anyone's interested, I thought Wimble showed himself to be a prime example of male chauvinist pig."

"You can't become a self-made millionaire without being one," Floyd remarked.

"What arrant nonsense!" Gwen exclaimed. "The two things have nothing to do with each other."

"If I may say so," Floyd said in a condescending tone, "that shows you don't know a great deal about the world of business."

"I can still recognise a male chauvinist pig when I see one."

"Anyway, what's being a male chauvinist pig got to do with this case?" Floyd enquired with a smirk.

"It indicates an attitude of mind, that's all."

"You'll be telling us next it's akin to the mark of Cain."

"You know, you're quite a one yourself," Gwen said with a sour little smile. "It takes one to defend another."

"Oh dear, why must they be so rude to each other?" Mrs. Norrington murmured to Reg Upham who was sitting on her other side.

"If he's a male chauvinist pig, she's the female equivalent," Reg replied with a chuckle. "Have a glance at our foreman's face, he looks like an early puritan at a roulette party."

Mrs. Norrington shook her head sadly. She had had no idea that being on a jury would produce such rancour. She had imagined it would be more like one of her coffee mornings in aid of the Red Cross.

"Don't be worried," Martin whispered into her other ear, "they won't come to blows."

She managed a frail smile. "I'm not worried so much as shocked. It's so unnecessary. Heaven knows what it'll be like when we actually come to consider our verdict!"

"I reckon we'll have quite a lively discussion if Hitler lets us."

"Hitler? Oh, really! You're very naughty to say that. I feel sorry for the poor man."

"No need to; he wanted the job. Nobody pushed him into it."

Aware that the foreman was staring at them across the table, she turned away in confusion and busied herself in a further examination of her lettuce.

"I'm always suspicious of salad I haven't prepared myself," she said to Reg Upham with a nervous smile.

"Call this salad," he said witheringly. "It's more like something salvaged from a rabbit's hutch."

"Oh, what a horrible thought!"

"But the pie's rather good," he went on, "except I had rather a small piece. Our young friend on your right fared much better. Ah well, another sacrifice for youth!"

On Reg's other side, Joyce Stanley was eating with a steady rhythmic motion of her lower jaw, which, from time to time, gave forth an ominous click.

"Is sitting on a jury what you expected it to be, Miss Stanley?" Reg enquired, determined to prise something out of her apart from a smile.

She stopped masticating, swallowed what was in her mouth and turned her gaze on him.

169

"It's exactly what I expected," she said in a low, husky voice.

"You sound as if you've done it before?"

She shook her head. "Not sitting on a jury," she said in a tantalising tone.

"I know, you've been a witness," Reg said promptly, intrigued to be actually holding a conversation with her.

She nodded. "That's right. I've been a witness."

"In a jury case?"

She nodded, her smile taking over again.

"You're from up north, aren't you? I'd say Liverpool at a guess."

"My parents came from there," she said in a tone that seemed to put an end to further conversation.

Funny, Reg thought, we were getting along quite nicely, too. She's certainly a rum one.

Meanwhile Joyce Stanley had crammed a lump of cheese into her mouth and was slowly chewing it. From the first day she had regarded Reg Upham as the most congenial of her fellow jurors and had wished he was sitting next to her in the jury box. Each day she had determined to talk to somebody, but the right person and moment had never seemed to coincide until now. Why did he have to go and mention Liverpool and send her scurrying to take refuge behind her meaningless smile?

She wondered how the accused was feeling as he sat in his cell beneath the court. The really testing time, of course, was when you were waiting for the jury's verdict. She remembered how her counsel had visited her and they had sat together in a glum silence until she suggested he should leave her, which he had done with obvious relief.

She had wondered whether a better counsel

would have got her off. He hadn't handled the case very well and seemed aware of it.

But then who was to know that the appeal court would seize on two sentences of the judge's summing-up and quash her conviction and sentence? She still felt bewildered when she thought about it. Life was enough of a gamble without the law fumbling with the dice.

And now here she was on the opposite side of the fence, without any fellow feeling for the man on trial. His crime and hers had but one thing in common. The descriptive label, murder.

Dinsford Crown Court had no canteen facilities and so every lunchtime saw an exodus of foraging lawyers and others. Heavily patronised were two public houses and a café on the opposite side of the road, with counsel favouring The Rising Sun which had a pleasant saloon bar and a good range of hot food suitable for eating with a fork, standing up if necessary.

Its smaller and more austere neighbour, The Stag's Head, supplied the jury's cold lunches. Tradition and a tight rein on public expenditure ensured that only juries in murder cases received such pampered treatment, though it is doubtful whether many of them would have chosen that word to describe it. Nevertheless, it did give them the feeling of being special and it was, of course, free.

Donlon and his junior usually managed to arrive ahead of the defending team. They liked to ensconce themselves in a corner where, if lucky, they were able to balance their food on a small, wobbly table.

By the time Coe and Stephen Kitter and their instructing solicitor arrived there were seldom any seats left and they would cram themselves against the far end of the bar.

171

Any stranger entering upon the scene could have been forgiven for thinking he had strayed into a room devoted to the hatching of sinister plots and conspiracies, for counsel were apt to give quick furtive glances about them before speaking. Not to take this precaution was a recipe for potential embarrassment as morsels of overheard conversation were liable to appear later in the press in a suitably laundered, but still identifiable, form. It had become such a habit with counsel that they often lowered their voices even when asking for the salt or the ketchup bottle.

"You'd better eat up or you'll be late," Alan Coe said to his junior, as he pushed his own empty plate away from him.

Stephen Kitter, who had a healthy appetite and always ordered the same thing, namely a double helping of shepherds pie, glanced anxiously at his watch and began to speed up the movement of his fork.

"I'm just going to have a word with Michael Donlon," Coe remarked, sliding off his bar stool and walking over to where Donlon and Kenneth Platman faced each other across the debris of their completed meal. After satisfying himself that there were no intrusive ears in the vicinity, he said, "How long do you reckon you'll be addressing the jury for, Michael?"

Donlon shifted uneasily. "Not much more than an hour, I'd say."

Knowing you, that means at least an hour and a half, Coe thought. He would normally have regarded this as an inordinately long closing speech for prosecuting counsel (his own reckoning when prosecuting was roughly ten minutes for each day of evidence), but as he had no wish to begin his own closing address on a Friday evening and then wait till

Monday to continue it, he was quite happy that his opponent should use up the afternoon. He thought there was a very good chance that, if Donlon didn't finish before four o'clock, the judge would adjourn a bit early and give him the advantage of a clear run on Monday.

"But you reckon you'll finish this afternoon?" he said.

"Certainly. Mind you, I don't like having a whole weekend intervening between my last word to the jury and their retirement. By the time Monday comes they won't remember a single thing I've said to them. It really isn't awfully satisfactory from the prosecution's point of view."

"It's a darned sight worse if it happens when you're defending," Coe said vigorously.

"I know that, but it's still unsatisfactory."

"You can rely on the judge to remember what you've said, even if the jury have forgotten."

"Which way do you think she's going to play it? I've only appeared in front of her once before and on that occasion she gave nothing away in the course of the trial, but gave me a proper hammering when she summed up."

"I have a great respect for Isabelle Gentry," Coe said. "She possesses a more judicial mind than some of her male colleagues and she never shows her feelings until the proper moment. Moreover, I've never known her be other than courtesy itself to witnesses and counsel alike."

"That's quite a testimonial," Donlon remarked thoughtfully. "Tell me, Alan, how would you sum up if you were trying this case?"

"Entirely pro defence," Coe said with a grin.

"No, seriously, how would you?"

"I'd play it straight down the middle and let the

jury decide it for themselves with minimum of comment from me. There aren't any legal issues to complicate matters, so that it becomes simply a question of what evidence they accept and what they reject and then drawing the necessary conclusions."

"Having said that, what do you think their verdict will be?"

Coe gave a short laugh. "If I could answer that I wouldn't be a grubbing lawyer. I'd be God himself."

18

Isabelle Gentry had not adjourned her court half an hour later than usual solely out of consideration for prosecuting counsel. There had also been a more personal motive.

Her brother-in-law, of whom she was very fond, had called her two nights earlier to say that he would be passing through Dinsford around lunchtime on Friday and how nice it would be to see her, though he realised that it was not a very convenient hour to visit a busy judge.

She had immediately asked him to have lunch with her at the lodgings, an invitation he had promptly accepted. However, when the next evening he telephoned again to say that he couldn't reach Dinsford before one thirty and must therefore reluctantly forgo the pleasure of a visit, she had said that that would be just as suitable. There was no point in being a high court judge, she had added, if you couldn't occasionally arrange things to please yourself.

"The public will still enjoy my services for the same number of hours," she had remarked drily.

Her brother-in-law, Tom, who was her dead husband's brother, was a director of a merchant bank and a potent figure in the world of Finance. He had been a great support to Isabelle in many ways since her husband's death.

"How very nice to see you, Isabelle," he said as he was shown into the drawing-room. She would have been happy to have gone and opened the front door for him, but feared that the butler might take it amiss.

"Do you mind if we eat straightaway, Tom? Judges' lunch hours are amongst the shortest in the land. But then we don't have to cook it ourselves or stand in a queue waiting to be served." She led the way into the dining-room where the butler was waiting to serve them. "The fact that I don't drink anything at lunchtime mustn't prevent you," she said, surveying the array of wine glasses on the table.

After the butler had retired, he remarked in an appreciative tone, "I'm glad to note that Her Majesty's judges are still properly looked after."

"We're certainly a pampered species on circuit. Personally, I find a little of it lasts a long time."

"You must get awfully tired of being endlessly on circuit. I"m sure I would."

"Yes and no. Fortunately, it's not endless. I spend quite a lot of time sitting at the Law Courts in London and doing the occasional stint at the Old Bailey. One meets a lot of nice people going on circuit, but the life can be a bit artificial with all the formal and semi-formal entertainment."

There was a brief silence while they ate. Then he said, "How are John and Peter?"

"I'm spending the weekend at Peter's," she said, and went on to tell him of her son's marital troubles.

"I'm very sorry to hear that," he said in a sympathetic tone. "I'd always looked upon them as happily married."

"So had I," she remarked wistfully. "It looks as if I shall spend most of the weekend entertaining Adam and Jane while Peter attempts to patch things up with Fran. Though it's really she who should do the patching."

"Anyway, I'm sure you'll enjoy the company of your grandchildren."

"I shall adore it. I just pray that they won't be the ones who suffer..."

They were finishing their coffee when the official Rolls arrived to convey her back to court.

"Sounds as if you're trying an interesting case," he remarked, as he watched her don her scarlet robe and adjust her wig and become Mrs. Justice Gentry again.

"Interesting, macabre and something of a puzzle," she said, as she picked up her handbag and made for the front door with her nautical gait. "Sorry to desert you like this, Tom," she called over her shoulder with a rueful smile. "I can't even offer you a lift."

On arriving back at court, she braced herself for an enervating afternoon. The drone of a monotonous voice could be as conducive to sleep as half a bottle of burgundy at lunch and Michael Donlon's delivery wasn't exactly lively. Moreover, there was something about Friday afternoons which tended to make the concentration waver.

In order that justice may not only be done, but be seen to be done, a judge needed to appear alert and in control all the time and Isabelle Gentry was very conscious of this. It was necessary, too, to be ready to intervene at a second's notice if counsel overstepped the mark in any way. Thus, others might safely doze off, but not the judge.

"Yes, Mr. Donlon," she said brightly on taking her seat, without any hint of what was going through her mind.

Prosecuting counsel rose, gave his gown an extra vigorous hitch and caressingly smoothed the pages of his open notebook.

"May it please your ladyship. Members of the jury, it now falls to me to address you on behalf of the prosecution and to sum up the case as we, the prosecution, suggest you should see it. You have now heard all the evidence on both sides and will shortly be considering your verdict.

"When I opened the case to you four days ago, I ventured to say that the story you were about to hear was as ancient as the Old Testament itself and as modern as a current crime novel. The age old story, in fact, of a man lusting after another woman and being driven to kill his own wife to satisfy his covetousness.

"In my submission, there is one key word to describe the defence in this case. Improvisation." He paused and let his gaze roam along the two rows of jurors. "Yes, improvisation. The accused has met each fresh development with an improvised response, only later to abandon it and improvise anew.

"Think back to that Saturday morning at the end of September last year when Mrs. Passingham arrived at Downview Lodge, expecting to find Mrs. Wimble. She has to be given some explanation for her absence, so what is she told? That Mrs. Wimble has been abruptly called away to the bedside of a sick aunt. The story was even embellished (unwisely as it turns out) to provide it with a touch of verisimilitude. 'I drove her into Dinsford,' the accused said to Mrs. Passingham, 'and she caught the last train to London.'

"Not a word of truth in any of that, as the accused has since been obliged to admit. Nevertheless, for the next two and a half months it was the only recorded explanation of her absence from home. It remained so until a Saturday morning in the middle of December when Police Constable Jameson called at the house.

"For some time the accused must have realised that what he had told Mrs. Passingham wouldn't stand up to examination if the police began to make enquiries. So what does he do? He abandons that story and, with what you may regard as a piece of brazen effrontery, admits to the officer that it isn't true and that he told it to save himself embarrassment. Faced with the prospect of police enquiries unless he can head them off, he once more improvises to meet this new situation. 'My wife,' he tells P.C. Jameson, 'has gone off with another man. I don't know who he is or where she has gone. She's left me. Deserted me.'

"You may think, members of the jury that, coming when it did, it was an extremely unlikely story. Nevertheless it, too, received a touch of embellishment in order to make it more credible. 'Three days after my wife's disappearance,' he says to the officer, 'she called me to say she had left me for good and that I would never see her again.' Have you ever heard such an improbable story?" Donlon's tone became heavy with sarcasm. "This woman, who walked out on her husband without a breath of warning and without so much as an overnight bag, takes the trouble to telephone him three days later simply to inform him that he'll never see her again. Can you really believe that? Or is it another piece of improvisation designed to forestall further police enquiries? Because, of course, if his wife was still alive, as he

179

wanted the police to believe, they would have taken no further interest in the matter. In the event it proved to be a short-lived attempt to throw them off the trail, but that, I suggest, was most certainly its purpose. For by then, members of the jury, if you accept the prosecution's interpretation of events, the accused must have been reasonably confident that no trace of his wife would ever be found. Two and a half months had gone by and his confidence would have been growing with each week that passed without the discovery of her body. In those circumstances, he reckoned he could safely offer this fresh explanation of her disappearance, namely that she had left him for ever and had thoughtfully telephoned to let him know.

"But the police are trained not to swallow everything they're told, members of the jury, and so enquiries continued and gathered weight. We can only speculate what the accused's thoughts must have been as he watched them dig up his garden and search every inch of the neighbourhood for traces of her. How close they came to finding her remains we don't know, but can you seriously doubt that she lies buried somewhere in that vicinity?

"And then we move forward to the end of March and the macabre discovery of her fleshless hand with her ring on the wedding finger.

"Confronted by that devastating piece of evidence further improvisation becomes necessary. This time, however, it is rather more devious. He doesn't make the bold assertions of before, but invites a subtle inference to be drawn. My wife, he says, had been behaving oddly. She was going for long walks after dark. She must have had an accident or been taken ill and died. She may even have decided to take her own life. In the first place, members of the jury, Dr.

Young, although called by the defence, hardly supported the picture of a neurotic woman on the verge of a major nervous breakdown. In the second, do you really believe her body would have gone undiscovered all this while if she had merely collapsed and died while out for a walk?" He leaned forward over his lectern to add emphasis to his words. "And if you don't believe that, what are you left with?" He seemed to glance at each juror in turn. "Surely there is only one conclusion, namely that the accused murdered his wife and disposed of her body, since when he has lied at every turn to try and conceal that grisly fact. Lied and improvised to meet each new set of circumstances.

"He certainly had the motive and the opportunity was there, too.

"He has made much of his revulsion at the sight of blood and you are asked to deduce from that that he couldn't have killed his wife. Well, as I pointed out to him in cross-examination, it's perfectly possible to commit murder without any spillage of blood. So, members of the jury, even if you accept that he does suffer from a certain squeamishness, even an excessive squeamishness if you will, it doesn't really do anything to rebut the logical and inevitable inferences the prosecution invite you to draw from the evidence."

Up to this point, Mrs. Justice Gentry had been more impressed by prosecuting counsel's speech than she had expected to be. But when he began to recapitulate and pop in bits that appeared suddenly to occur to him, she found herself fidgeting. Twice he seemed about to sit down, but on each occasion started up again. It was as if he felt he had overlooked something and would remember what it was if he continued talking long enough.

181

At last, however, he reached what proved to be his final peroration.

"Members of the jury, I have now addressed you on those matters which the prosecution suggest you ought to have in mind when considering your verdict. It is, of course, as my lady will direct you, for the prosecution to prove its case to your satisfaction. You are not required to be mathematically certain of the accused's guilt, merely as sure as you would wish to be before reaching a decision on some important matter in your everyday lives.

"When you take the evidence as a whole, members of the jury, are you left in any reasonable doubt as to the accused's guilt? In my submission, the prosecution has proved its case and you should convict the accused of the murder of his wife, Elspeth Wimble, in September last year."

Mrs. Justice Gentry waited until he had completely sat down before making any move.

"Thank you, Mr. Donlon," she said. Then after glancing at the clock, she directed her gaze at Alan Coe. "It's five minutes past four, Mr. Coe. You obviously can't finish in the time now left and, in those circumstances, I imagine that you would sooner defer starting your speech until Monday morning?"

"I would certainly prefer to adopt that course if it's convenient to your ladyship."

She swivelled round to address the jury. "I don't suppose," she said with a smile, "that any of you will mind if the court adjourns a bit early on a Friday evening. Then when we resume on Monday all that will be left before you retire to consider your verdict will be Mr. Coe's closing speech and my summing-up. I think I can safely say that the trial should finish on Tuesday. Having said that, however, let me add that you will be under no pressure of time and that you can take as long as you wish to reach a verdict. One further matter before we disperse. At this stage of the trial and with the weekend ahead of us, it is more important than ever that you should keep your own counsel. Allow no one to try and influence you, and refuse to discuss the case with your family or friends."

She pushed back her chair and everyone stood up. The usher intoned his piece and, after bows all round, she left the bench, her mind already focused on what she could expect to find when she reached her son's home later that evening.

19

"Grannie, come and look at the picture I've drawn you," Jane said excitedly, clutching her grandmother's hand and tugging her in the direction of their playroom.

From her other side, Adam asked gravely, "Is it true, grannie, that judges can have someone locked up just for putting out his tongue in court?"

The children had been waiting for her arrival and had flung open the front door before she had time to ring the bell.

"Where's daddy?" she asked, allowing herself to be steered into the playroom.

"He's somewhere upstairs," Adam said. "You haven't answered my question, grannie. Can they?"

"I drew this specially for you," Jane said, thrusting into her hand a picture in which a thousand and one things seemed to be going on at the same time. "Do you like it?"

"Very much, darling. It's so full of detail."

"Can they, grannie?" Adam asked in a tone of quiet patience.

"If it amounted to what is called contempt of

court, they could be. But it very rarely happens. Anyway, who told you that?"

"A boy at school. His uncle was locked up just because the judge didn't like him."

"That I won't believe, Adam."

"It's true, grannie. Weaver said so."

"You ask Weaver what his uncle was doing in court in the first place," she remarked with a smile.

"I think he just happened to be there," Adam said with a slight frown.

"I'm sorry, mum, I was upstairs when you arrived." Peter came across the room and gave his mother a kiss. "Come into the drawing-room and let me get you a drink."

"Can I come, too?" Jane asked eagerly.

"No. You and Adam play in here until supper's ready."

"Oh, daddy, that's not fair. We hardly ever see grannie."

"If you want to stay up for supper, you'd better stop whining. Anyway, grannie'll be here all tomorrow and most of Sunday, so you'll see lots of her."

"Can I go up and see mummy then?" Jane asked.

Isabelle Gentry cast her son a startled look.

"No. She'll be down shortly. She's just having a few minutes rest."

"Grown-ups are always resting," Jane said witheringly.

Peter took his mother into the drawing-room and closed the door behind him. "She came back this afternoon," he said in answer to her unspoken question.

"How is she?"

"A bit edgy at the moment, but I think everything will be all right. The important thing is that she's returned of her own accord."

"Did you know she was coming back?"

He shook his head. "She was here when I arrived home. Apparently it was a spur of the moment decision on her part."

"Have you been able to talk to her?"

"No. She obviously didn't want to discuss what had happened and it wasn't the moment for reproaches or showdowns."

"Did she say why she'd come back?"

"I think she was missing the children a lot and perhaps me a bit."

"What about the neighbour?"

He gave a shrug. "Sometime we'll obviously have to try and sort out that situation. In the meantime, however, she's back and that's what matters most."

At that moment the door opened and the object of their discussion came in.

"Fran, dear, how nice to see you!" Isabelle exclaimed as she went across to greet her daughter-in-law.

"I heard the children setting on you almost before you were through the front door," Fran said with a wan smile. "You're much better with them than my own mother. She overawes them."

"A lot of people would say that too few children are overawed these days and more's the pity. Incidentally, how is your mother?"

Fran gave her mother-in-law a wry look. "In the rudest of health."

"I ought to have told you, Fran," Peter broke in, "I explained your absence to the children by telling them your mother had been taken ill."

She nodded. "I gathered that from what they said when I got back. I've told them that she's now well again."

"Would you like a drink?" he asked.

Why couldn't he just hand her one without asking, Isabelle thought with a sigh, instead of sounding like a polite host with a shy guest?

"Yes, please. But very little gin and mostly tonic."

For the next fifteen minutes they touched on almost every topic save the one that was uppermost in all their minds. Then Fran put down her empty glass and got up.

"I'd better go and organise supper." she said.

"Is Heidi in?" Isabelle enquired, referring to their au pair.

"Yes, but she'll need a hand. Especially as Peter has told the children they can eat with us in honour of your visit."

"Shall I come and help?"

"No, you stay and talk to Peter. It won't take me long."

I've simply got to have a heart-to-heart talk with her, Isabelle reflected as she watched her daughter-in-law leave the room. I don't want to be an interfering mother-in-law, but I can't spend the weekend avoiding the one subject that matters.

Thanks to the children's incessant prattle supper passed off without embarrassment, despite Peter's somewhat stiffish manner and Fran's distant looks.

As soon as the meal was over, Adam and Jane were packed off to bed with a promise from their mother that she would come up and say good night to them in ten minutes time.

"Can grannie come, too?" Jane asked.

"Grannie's had a long and busy day and I'm sure she'd sooner go and sit down," Fran replied.

"But she's been sitting down all day," Jane exclaimed. "Judges spend all their time sitting down. Oh, do come, grannie!"

Isabelle gave her daughter-in-law a questioning glance.

"By all means come up if you're not too tired," Fran said in the same rather subdued tone in which she had spoken the whole evening.

Later, after kissing her grandchildren good night, Isabelle went to her own room to do a quick running repair to her face.

She had her back to the open door when she heard Fran speak.

"May I come in, Isabelle? I'd better make sure the bed is all right and Heidi has put you some clean towels." With one of her wan smiles, she added, "I know the good hostess does it *before* her guest arrives."

Isabelle studied her daughter-in-law in silence for a moment.

"I'm so relieved you're back, Fran," she said with a faint tremor in her voice. "Peter was desolate when I talked to him last Tuesday and I know the children would soon have begun to miss you terribly."

For several seconds Fran stared at her with a distant expression. Then she gave a small nod and said, "Well, I'm back now."

"I realise that the next few weeks are not going to be easy for either you or Peter, but I pray that you'll be able to make your marriage work again for the sake of the children."

"They're why I came back," she said, with a note of defiance.

"I can well understand that. Look, Fran, I don't wish to be nosier than I ought to be, but are you out of love with Peter? Is that the root of the problem?"

"I'm still very fond of him," she said in a flat voice.

"But you find this other man more exciting, is that it?"

"In a way."

"Don't think I'm blaming you, because I'm sure Peter must share the responsibility for what's happened. The faults seldom lie all on one side." Observing Fran's faintly suspicious glance, she went on, "I'm not being devious when I say that. I mean it, even if he is my own son. I just hope he will have the wit to recognise it and apply the right remedy, though I'm pretty sure he will." She paused and gave her daughter-in-law a compassionate look. "I suppose you can't easily avoid running into this other man, seeing that he lives nearby and his children go to the same school as Jane, and that's bound to make things more difficult for you."

A silence fell between them, then Fran said, "I won't try and forecast how the future will work out, but let's hope..."

"Fran, dear, it's no use just hoping. You'll both have to work hard at your marriage if it's not to founder. And should that happen, Adam and Jane will be the victims. Adam and Jane, who never asked to be brought into this world, will suffer because their parents didn't try sufficiently hard to make a go of their marriage."

Fran grimaced. "It can be worse for children to live with endlessly rowing parents," she said with a note of challenge.

"I agree, but Adam and Jane don't live in that sort of poisoned atmosphere and I'm sure you and Peter would never inflict it on them."

Fran smiled faintly. "That sounds like a piece of special pleading."

"It's the plea of an adoring grandmother."

At that moment Jane called out in her sleep and Fran, after listening attentively for a second cry, tiptoed along to her daughter's room.

The next day Isabelle had a chance of a similar talk to her son when Fran went to the shops just before lunch, taking the children with her. It was as if she wished to provide her mother-in-law with the opportunity of playing a mediator's role and Isabelle was ready to take it.

Peter listened to her, but said very little himself. His mood seemed neither euphoric nor depressed, which made his mother infer that, given the chance, time would play its part. He had apparently judged it best not to rush things.

Nevertheless, when she departed around six o'clock on Sunday evening, she felt considerably more hopeful than she had on arrival forty-eight hours earlier. If her hopes were still somewhat restrained that was partly a lawyer's training and partly because she had seen too much of life for them not to be.

20

Graham Tapling forwent his usual Sunday morning golf and visited his client in prison instead. He was motivated not so much by a sense of professional duty as by a desire to keep in with a client who supplied him with so much lucrative work. And, he hoped, would continue to do so.

Frank Wimble was surprised to see his solicitor and said so.

"It's really a social visit, Frank," Tapling remarked pleasantly. "I know that prison can be a dreary place on a Sunday, especially at this stage of a trial, and I decided you might like a bit of company from the outside world."

"I didn't think yesterday would ever end. It was the longest day I've lived."

"Well, by this time next week it'll all be over."

"Yes, but where'll I be?"

"I very much hope you'll be a free man."

"You still think I stand a good chance of getting off?"

"A very reasonable chance."

"Is that Coe's view as well?"

"He's also not without hope."

"All you bloody lawyers are the same. You hedge all the time."

Tapling smiled good-naturedly. "We have to. Especially where juries are concerned."

"I still don't like the look of some of my jury. Supposing they don't agree?"

"There'll have to be a retrial."

"When?"

"As soon as possible..."

"Meanwhile, I suppose I'm shut up in this bloody prison."

"Let's take one thing at a time, Frank," Tapling said soothingly. "There's no point in worrying about retrials until we're obliged to."

"Know what I'm going to do when it's all over?" Wimble said after a brief silence. "I shall throw a great party at Downview Lodge. I shall ask all the locals to show them I've not run away and hidden my face. It'll prove to them I always believed in my own innocence and had nothing to conceal. You'll get an invitation, of course."

"I'll look forward to it," the solicitor remarked drily. "But surely you'll have a holiday first?"

"Might take Maureen over to Paris for a long weekend later on, but I'll need to be back at my desk as soon as the case is over. That'll show everyone." In a dreamy tone, he added, "To think it could be in three days' time..." Returning his gaze to his solicitor, he said briskly, "I'll want you to arrange a press conference. There's a whole lot I intend the world to know."

"We can discuss that later," Tapling said quickly. "First things first."

He could foresee life being equally troublesome whether his client was acquitted or convicted.

As for Frank Wimble himself, he had moved into a realm in which he didn't so much delude himself that he was innocent as that he deserved to be acquitted.

21

Unlike his instructing solicitor, Alan Coe did play a round of golf on Sunday morning, but spent the rest of the day preparing his final speech. It was a case where he felt his client had a very fair chance of acquittal and this increased his own feeling of responsibility. Nothing must be left unsaid and thorough preparation was the only way of ensuring that.

Mrs. Justice Gentry had an almost jaunty air as she came on the bench on Monday morning. The old dear obviously had a good weekend, Coe reflected.

From appearance, the jury could have spent theirs shut away in a box like toys and have been only brought out again to be played with that morning. The judge gave them a quick appraising glance before indicating to defending counsel that he could begin.

"May it please your ladyship. When my learned friend opened this case to you last Tuesday, members of the jury, he said in one of his more picturesque phrases that it was a story as ancient as the Old Testament itself and he repeated the metaphor when he addressed you again on Friday afternoon. You may have a clearer idea than I of what he meant, but one thing is certainly apparent, namely that the word story is the right one for describing the case for the prosecution. Story in the sense of a fable or a piece of fiction.

"When you come to analyse the prosecution's evidence, I suggest that you find it consists of so many strands of gossamer suspicion linked to a few hard facts.

"But before I come to deal with it in detail, allow me to dispose of one matter. This, members of the jury, is a criminal court and you have ben empanelled to try the accused on a specific charge, namely murder. You are not here to pass judgment on his morals. You may disapprove of men who keep mistresses, you may think the accused treated his wife badly in this respect, but you must not let such feelings affect your judgment when considering the evidence. His morals are not on trial in this court.

"Now, I'd like to return to my main theme.

"Great play has been made of the lies told by the accused to Mrs. Passingham and to P.C. Jameson. As far as Mrs. Passingham is concerned, I ask you to say that what he told her was nothing worse than a white lie. We are all prone to tell white lies, usually on the spur of the moment and with the object of covering up our embarrassment. Isn't that exactly the position here? He has to tell Mrs. Passingham something and so, on the spur of the moment, says his wife has been called away to a sick aunt. There was nothing sinister in telling that untruth and he later made no attempt to sustain it. It was an everyday white lie and I ask you so to view it.

"As for what he said to P.C. Jameson, it wasn't a lie at all, for, at the time, he seriously believed his wife *had* deserted him and *was* alive. My learned friend asks you to say that the telephone call he received from his wife shortly after her disappearance is an invention on his part and that it never took place. Well, the only *evidence* bearing on the subject is what the accused himself has told you and he says she *did* call him.

"Next we come to all those searches made by the police of his house and garden. Searches which he welcomed and willingly consented to. For mark you, members of the jury, had he not consented, the police would have had no right to carry them out. Detective Superintendent Barty grudgingly admitted this, but implied darkly that if the accused hadn't agreed, the police would have found some way round the difficulty. Maybe they would have, but one wonders whether it would have been a legal path they'd have trodden... At all events, they were saved recourse to their other means by the accused's cooperation. Does that look to you to be the action of a guilty man with much to hide or was it more that of an innocent person who was ready to do everything he could to have himself cleared of suspicion?

"As I understand the prosecution's case, you are being invited to infer that when Dr. Farrer saw the accused drive out of Downview Lodge in the early hours of that Saturday morning, he, the accused, was on his way to dispose of the already dead body of his wife. They don't tell you how he had killed her, because there's no evidence that he ever did so. On the other hand, you do have evidence (even from his own son who is not exactly on good terms with his father) that the accused couldn't stand the sight of blood. My learned friend rather glibly suggests that he may have poisoned her, but the prosecution hasn't produced an iota of evidence to support that suggestion. And you may be quite sure, members of the jury, that if they could have, they would have. Moreover, it's clear that these searches of the accused's home failed to reveal any evidence of murder having been committed there and exhaustive examination by experts from the forensic science laboratory also produced nothing.

"Nevertheless, you are asked by the prosecution to infer that he did kill her and that he was on his way to bury her body when Dr. Farrer happened to come along in his car.

"The accused has given you his explanation of why he was out that night. On the spur of the moment and in something of a panic, he decided to go and search for his wife in the surrounding lanes. It was a futile exercise, as he quickly realised, but it was nonetheless a perfectly plausible act in the circumstances.

"You are next asked to draw the most mind-stretching inference of all, namely that he so successfully disposed of her body that six months passed before the first real evidence of her death came to light with the discovery of her hand by a dog.

"Members of the jury, you are invited by the prosecution to say that this was a most cunningly devised and cleverly executed crime. And yet this criminal mastermind left his wife's wedding ring on her finger so that she could be instantly identified. Her body might rot away, but not her gold wedding ring."

After a significant pause he went on, "It doesn't make sense, does it? And yet that's what you are being asked to believe. He might just as well have left a signed note saying, 'I did it.'

"On the other hand, it makes much better sense if you accept the more plausible and likely inference that she somehow came by her own death while out for one of her solitary walks.

"The defence can't tell you exactly what happened any more than the prosecution can (and it is the prosecution on whom lies the burden of proving the charge), but don't you think that's a far more acceptable inference? Namely, that this unfortunate woman died by misadventure or conceivably by her own deliberate act? It would explain why her wedding ring was still on her finger.

"Just consider for a moment the unhappy scenario against which her death must be seen. Her husband had fallen in love with another woman whom he wished to marry. He had been pressing his wife to give him a divorce which she had refused to do. As you will have gathered, members of the jury, he is not the sort of man who readily accepts refusal. He argued and no doubt put great pressure on her to do what he wanted. In those circumstances, it's not difficult, is it, to imagine the tension building up inside his wife. Tension such as to undermine natural health and distort her perspective. And that's precisely what happened to Mrs. Wimble. Her pattern of life changed; her personality changed as she became less communicative and ever more solitary. She began to take long walks in the dark countryside. I accept that Dr. Young has said he didn't consider she was on the verge of a nervous breakdown. I suppose it may depend on how you define the word verge, but you may take the view, members of the jury, that she can't have been very far off one in late September last year.

"And so we come to that Friday when she disappeared. She knows that her husband is coming home for the weekend and that all she can look forward to is more argument, more pressure, more strain and yet more tension. Not a happy prospect. So what more likely than that she should go off for one of her walks, which, one imagines, had a therapeutic effect? It may be possible to deduce that she left home some hours before her husband's expected arrival, for, as we've heard, she hadn't started to make any preparations for their evening meal. Either that or she never had any intention of returning home, having already decided to end her life.

"In my submission, members of the jury, either of those alternatives is more credible than anything the prosecution has advanced.

"Without knowing what was her exact state of mind that Friday evening, I'm not in a position to say that one alternative is more likely than the other, that is to say whether she died by misadventure or of her own self-made choice. From the fact that no trace of her has ever been found apart from her left hand, you may incline to the view that she chose her own place to die rather than being overtaken by illness or an accident when there would have been a greater likelihood of the discovery of her body.

"But what I do unhesitatingly submit to you is that the idea of this man having killed his wife and secretly disposed of her body is fanciful and beyond any stretch of the imagination."

Having reached this stage of his closing speech, Alan Coe proceeded to deal with the evidence of each prosecution witness in turn, subjecting it, where possible, to corrosive scorn or, at the very least, seeking to neutralise it.

It seemed to Mrs. Justice Gentry that at times he was in risk of being carried away by his own rhetoric, though he appeared to sustain the attention of the jury. But then juries were always more receptive on Monday mornings than Friday afternoons.

It was after half past twelve when he finally sat

down and she decided to adjourn early, rather than break off her summing-up in its preliminaries.

"We'll resume at a quarter to two," she announced after a moment's thoughtful study of the court-room clock.

22

The atmosphere was subdued as the jury sat down to their lunch that day, induced by a consciousness that the case would shortly pass into their hands for decision. Only Peter Floyd seemed unaffected by the general air of impending responsibility.

"You'd have thought they'd have given us something special for our last meal together," he said, eyeing his leg of cold chicken with disfavor. "I'm not saying we should have fillet of steak or sole veronique, but just something different from this. My bit of chicken is almost as fleshless as Mrs. Wimble's hand."

"What a revolting thing to say!" Gwen Hackford exclaimed. "Anyway, what makes you so certain it is our last meal together?"

"Surely it'll all be over by this time tomorrow?" Floyd said in a tone of dismay. "It must be. I've made a number of appointments for the afternoon."

"I doubt whether the judge will complete her summing-up today and even if we retire in mid-morning, we're unlikely to have reached a verdict by lunchtime."

"Why on earth not? I imagine most of us already have a pretty good idea how we're going to vote. Supposing we each take five minute to say our piece, it only adds up to an hour." He paused and said in meaningful tone, "And some of us won't even take five minutes."

Gwen gave him a pitying look. "You're being rather naive if you think our discussion is going to be like a television debate with so many minutes per person."

Mr. Hislop now chimed in with a note of reproof. "I would remind you that the judge has already said we can have as long as we wish to consider our verdict and that we mustn't feel ourselves under any pressure of time."

Floyd gave an irritable shrug. "Well, I just hope I'm not the only person in the room who thinks we can comfortably reach a verdict in an hour."

He glanced round the table, but learnt nothing from the expressions of his fellow jurors, whose concentration seemed to be focused on their plates. Even Martin Capper, whom he regarded as a sure ally, failed to rally to his support.

When the jury bailiff arrived to conduct them back to court, they followed him like silent pilgrims nearing the grail.

23

As soon as Mrs. Justice Gentry took her seat on the bench that afternoon, she turned to face the jury.

"Let me begin, members of the jury, by directing you on a general principle of law that applies to all criminal cases. It is that burden of proof rests upon the prosecution. Both counsel have been at pains to tell you that, but it doesn't exempt me, as judge, from repeating it. Now let me explain the standard of proof required before you are entitled to convict. It is that you must be satisfied beyond reasonable doubt of the accused's guilt before you can find him guilty. A reasonable doubt is the sort of doubt that might affect your minds in the conduct of important affairs. Another way of putting it is that you must be satisfied so as to feel sure of his guilt. And if you are not thus satisfied, the accused has the right to be found not guilty.

"The next thing I wish to tell you is that you, and you alone, are the judges of fact. You must accept my direction on any matters of law, but the facts are solely within your province. Should I happen to express a view of the facts with which you disagree, it is your view, not mine, that counts.

"The charge in this case is murder, which is defined as the unlawful killing of another person with malice aforethought, either express or implied. That in essence means killing either with an intent to kill or with intent to cause serious injury; what the law calls grievous bodily harm."

She gave them a smile which seemed to say, with me so far?

"Your task in this case is made simpler by the absence of any additional issues. Often in murder cases, juries are called upon to consider such matters as provocation or self-defence or diminished responsibility. None of those have reared their heads in this trial and there is no evidence whatsoever to justify your consideration of any such issue.

"Here you have a single, clear-cut issue. Did the accused murder his wife, as alleged by the prosecution? Or did he, as the defence invite you to say, have no part at all in bringing about her death?

"Which brings me to what I suggest should be your starting point when you come to consider your verdict. Are you satisfied on the evidence adduced by the prosecution that Elspeth Wimble is dead? Because, if that hasn't been proved to your satisfaction, the case collapses.

"Before we consider together what evidence there is relating to her death, let me say something about circumstantial evidence. In criminal cases it is rare to have the positive testimony of eye witnesses and therefore juries are often required to infer from the facts proved other facts which are necessary to establish guilt or innocence. Moreover, it has frequently been said that circumstantial evidence is the best evidence, being capable of proving a fact more accurately than direct testimony.

"Having said that, let us consider the evidence adduced by the prosecution to prove the death of Elspeth Wimble. First, there is the fleshless hand found some six months after her disappearance and some eight miles from Downview Lodge, Little Misten, where the Wimbles lived. On the wedding finger of the hand was a gold ring and on the inside band of that ring was the inscription FW to EW 11 July 1953. Brian Wimble has identified it as his mother's wedding ring by the two sets of initials and by the date which was his parents' wedding day." She gave the jury a smile as she went on, "Strictly speaking he is not the best witness to prove the date of his parents' wedding, but there's been no dispute that it was on that day and so you will probably feel it safe to accept that the ring in question was his mother's. If so, it provides a strong inference that the hand on which it was found was Elspeth Wimble's. Indeed, nobody has suggested otherwise, though that doesn't absolve you from giving the matter your own consideration.

"Once you are satisfied that the hand is that of Mrs. Wimble, it's a relatively short step to draw the further inference that she is dead.

"Thus far you may feel it is fairly plain sailing, but now you have to approach the central issue in this case. If she is dead, how did she die?

"There being no direct testimony to help you decide that question, you must look at all the surrounding circumstances.

"The first circumstance for your consideration is her abrupt and sudden disappearance sometime during the latter part of Friday the twenty-eighth of September or the early hours of the following morning. She had not apparently told anyone she was going away. She just vanished, one could almost say into thin air. That in itself seems remarkable, but even more remarkable is the fact that she appears to have left without taking anything with her. This didn't, however, prevent the accused telling Mrs. Passingham on Saturday morning that his wife had been called urgently to the bedside of a sick aunt. He has since admitted this was untrue and said that his only thought at the time was to avoid having to answer embarrassing questions. Of course, if you accept the prosecution's case, any questions would have been embarrassing at that moment. At all events he seems to have been successful in stemming such curiosity as Mrs. Passingham showed in her employer's disappearance.

"You will have to consider that lie he told Mrs. Passingham and decide whether you find his explanation of it acceptable.

"Some two months later he tells Police Constable Jameson that he now knows his wife has left him and he mentions the phone call he says he received from her shortly after her disappearance. The only evidence of that call comes from the accused himself and you must consider whether or not you believe his testimony on that point. Do you think it probable that, having walked out on her husband without warning or preparation, she would phone him a few days later? If you find it difficult to believe that phone call took place, then you have to ask yourselves why he should have invented it.

"You see, members of the jury, it's only by considering all the surrounding circumstances of his wife's disappearance that you can begin to draw the correct inferences as to how she came by her death. And in this same connection you have to decide how you regard the accused's failure to report her disappearance to the police. Was that a reasonable failure or was it that of a man who had something to conceal?

"Indeed, you have to consider the whole of the accused's conduct on that Friday evening when, as he tells you, he arrived home to find his wife missing. There was the initial quick search, followed by the drink. Then the sleep in his chair, after which he drove round the dark lanes looking for her. Finally he returned home, had another drink and retired to bed. In that whole chain of events there is, you may think, one sequence at odds with the rest. I refer to the taking out of his car and the driving around the local roads. He described it as something of a panic reaction, the futility of which he quickly realised. Of course, having been seen out by Dr. Farrer, he was obliged to provide an explanation and you have to consider whether it's a plausible one in the circumstances. The prosecution invite you to infer that his wife's body was in the car and that he was on his way to dispose of it.

"But supposing you reach the conclusion that Mrs. Wimble is, indeed, dead and furthermore that the accused has been less than truthful on various occasions when explaining or accounting for her disappearance, is that sufficient to justify the inference he murdered her, remembering, as you must at all times, that it is for the prosecution to prove his guilt beyond reasonable doubt and not for the accused to establish his innocence?

"The defence invite you to draw quite different inferences as to her death and in a moment I shall be reminding you of the evidence given by the witnesses on both sides..."

Alan Coe turned and whispered to his instructing solicitor, "She thinks he did it, but that the evidence falls short."

Mr. Tapling nodded. "Let's hope the jury think so, too. I mean that the evidence falls short," he added quickly.

The accused, meanwhile, leaned forward listening with frowning attention to every nuance of the judge's words. Occasionally he glanced toward the jury in an attempt to read their minds. There was a hard glitter in his eyes, indicating an awareness that somehow he had to come out on top.

By the time the afternoon reached its end, the judge had all but completed her summing-up.

"Members of the jury," she said with a faintly weary smile, "I won't conclude my remarks to you until tomorrow morning, which means you will be able to retire with virtually the whole day ahead of you to consider your verdict."

There followed an even stronger exhortation than usual not to allow anybody to sully their minds by discussing the case outside the court's four walls.

When at ten thirty the next day she took her seat on the bench, she didn't bother to open her notebook or uncap her pen.

"Members of the jury, I now ask you to retire and consider your verdict. If the prosecution has proved its case beyond reasonable doubt, then it will be your duty to return a verdict of guilty. If they have failed to discharge that burden of proof, the accused is entitled to be acquitted. Those are the only two verdicts you have to consider. Please now do so."

Part 3

1

This time the places round the jury room table were laid with notepads and pencils, instead of plates of cold chicken, and the jurors brought with them the albums of photographs which they had had in court since the first day.

"Well, who's going to start the ball rolling?" Peter Floyd enquired when they were all seated.

Mr. Hislop frowned. Such flippancy was not befitting the occasion over which he was about to preside.

"I was going to propose," he said gravely, "that we should have a controlled discussion and that we should start where the judge suggested, namely with the death of Mrs. Wimble." He glanced from face to face, gratified by the attention he was receiving. "May I take it that we are all satisfied she *is* dead?"

Most of the jurors nodded solemnly and Floyd said, "There can't be any doubt about that, so let's get on to your next point."

"I'm not so sure," Martin Capper remarked boldly, in a tone that belied his nervousness.

"Not sure about what, Martin?" Floyd enquired.

"That we can take it for granted she's dead."

"I'm not taking anything for granted," Gwen Hackford said sharply.

"You mean you agree with Martin?"

"No. I merely repudiate his suggestion that I might be taking something for granted."

The foreman, having failed to secure order by clearing his throat, now tapped on the table with his pencil in the manner of a testy judge.

"We shall never achieve anything if we all talk at once," he said in a severe tone. Turning to Martin he went on, "Perhaps you'd explain your doubts, Mr. Capper."

"I've thought quite a lot about this," Martin said, moistening his lips which had become suddenly dry. "If she left home in such a hurry and without taking anything with her..."

"I don't remember anyone saying she left in a hurry," Gwen broke in.

"Well, she left suddenly and she certainly didn't stop to pack a bag. But do you remember how the accused told P.C. Jameson that he reckoned she hadn't taken any of her clothes with her because she wanted to make a complete break with the past and start life afresh? Do you all remember that? Well, if that's right, do you think it likely she would have hung on to her wedding ring of all things? I believe she suddenly realised it was still on her finger and just threw it away. Somebody could have found it and put it on their own finger..."

"And then had their hand chopped off, I suppose," Floyd remarked sardonically. "You've been watching too much television, Martin."

"There isn't a scrap of evidence to support your theory," Gwen observed. "It strikes me as too high-flown for words."

"What I've never understood," Mrs. Norrington

said in a puzzled voice, "is why she didn't take her car if she was really leaving her husband. I mean, you'd hardly expect her to set off on foot if that was her intention."

"She could have been traced more easily in her car," Reg Upham observed, "and I expect she'd have wanted to avoid that." He smiled slowly. "Not that I believe that is what happened. In fact, I think the suggestion that she upsticked and left her husband is a load of old rubbish."

"We do seem to have strayed rather a long way from Mr. Capper's point," Mr. Hislop said with a note of exasperation. "I'd like to dispose of it before we move on. Does anyone support Mr. Capper's theory that Mrs. Wimble could still be alive?"

Nobody spoke and Floyd said, "Bad luck, Martin, but it's a bit too much to swallow."

"I still think it's a possibility," Martin said, the corners of his mouth turned down in a temporary sulk.

"Anything's possible, old son. It's what is probable that counts," Floyd remarked. "Let's get on to the next point."

"Are you satisfied, Mr. Capper?" the foreman enquired.

"I reserve the right to raise it again later," Martin said stiffly.

"If everyone does that, we'll be here all tomorrow and the next day as well," Peter Floyd said.

"I'm entitled to my view."

"Nobody says you're not, but you have to pay a bit of attention to other people's."

"May I move on?" Mr. Hislop asked in a grating tone. "I suggest that the next matter we should discuss is the state of Mrs. Wimble's health at the time of her disappearance."

213

"Why on earth that?" Gwen asked. "It'd be much more to the point to discuss why the accused was so evasive afterwards. It seems to me his whole behaviour was that of a guilty man."

"But guilty of what?" Floyd enquired in a teasing voice.

"Of killing his wife, of course."

"How do you think he did it?" Reg Upham asked, while their foreman sat with an expression of pent-up frustration.

"Ah! That's what we have to discuss," Gwen said. "Personally, I don't believe all that nonsense about fainting at the sight of blood. I think it's grossly exaggerated and if he had wanted to be rid of his wife badly enough, he'd have put up with a bit of blood."

"That's flying in the face of the evidence if anything is," Floyd remarked with a faint note of jeer.

"And surely they'd have found signs of blood in the house?" Mrs. Norrington said.

"They'd have been all cleaned up by the time anyone came to look," Reg Upham said.

"But Mrs. Passingham was there the next morning," Mrs. Norrington protested. "She'd have noticed something."

"Because she didn't mention seeing anything suspicious, I assume there wasn't anything," Reg said. "Don't forget, the accused had the whole night to clear up his dirty work."

"There'd still have been damp patches," Mrs. Norrington persisted.

"Perhaps we could now get back to the deceased's state of mind," Mr. Hislop said in a despairing voice. "I suggest it's a most relevant issue for our consideration."

"Well, I personally don't believe for one moment that she committed suicide," Gwen remarked. "The suggestion that she went and lay down and waited to die of exposure is one of the silliest I've ever heard. If she'd wanted to commit suicide, there were a dozen quicker and easier ways."

"I entirely agree," Floyd said.

"People do rum things," Reg Upham remarked in a ruminative tone. "I had a great-uncle who first had to break the ice on a pond in order to drown himself."

"All I can say is, you wouldn't catch a woman doing anything as daft," Gwen retorted. "With all respect to your great-uncle, of course," she added quickly.

"Is it the general view that she was not of such a state of mind as to take her own life?" Mr. Hislop now asked.

"Poor woman, she must have been under a terrible strain," Mrs. Norrington observed.

"But do you think she committed suicide?"

"I don't like to think so."

"Does anyone think she did?" Mr. Hislop asked, glancing round the table.

"How can we possibly know?" Martin said.

"We have to try and form a view, Mr. Capper."

"Personally, I don't believe she either killed herself or died by misadventure."

"You mean, you think her husband murdered her?" Floyd asked.

"Yes."

"That hardly accords with your earlier belief that she threw away her wedding ring and could still be alive," Gwen remarked in her most acerbic tone.

"All I said was that I think he probably killed his wife. I never said I was satisfied beyond reasonable doubt," Martin replied with a faint air of smugness. "Personally, I find the case riddled with doubt."

"That's the purpose of discussion, to resolve our doubts," Mr. Hislop said.

"I don't see that it can."

"Perhaps if you sat and listened more to other people's views..."

"You're not my headmaster now," Martin said angrily, while Mr. Hislop compressed his lips into a thin outraged line.

"Why don't we take a vote now and see where we stand?" Floyd broke in. "It could save a lot of time."

"Do you mean on whether he's guilty or not?" Gwen asked with a frown.

"Why not? If we're already agreed, we needn't prolong our discussion. What about it, Mr. Foreman?"

Mr. Hislop, who was still trying to regain his inner composure after the dent Martin had given it, seemed to be uncertain what to do.

"Isn't it a bit premature?" he muttered. "But if we do take a vote now, I think it ought to be made clear that it's only a preliminary one and doesn't preclude further discussion."

"There'll be no point in further discussion if it's unanimous," Floyd said hopefully.

"If," Mr. Hislop said, with an apparent return of self-importance. He glanced down at the slip of paper on which he had recorded the names of his fellow jurors.

"Mr. Foster Jones?"

The juror in question gave a violent start. "I've not yet made up my mind," he stammered, as Peter Floyd rolled his eyes in despair.

"Mr. Farmiloe?"

"Nor have I."

"Mr. Whiting?"

"I don't think he's guilty, but I could be persuaded otherwise."

"Mr. Maxwell?"

"I'm afraid I'm a bit deaf, so I'd like to hear what others think first."

"*Hear*, did he say?" Floyd muttered in a sardonic aside to Martin.

"Miss Lipp?"

"Let's have a bit more discussion."

"Mrs. Stanley?"

"Not guilty."

"You've made up your mind already?" Mr. Hislop said, reflecting the general air of surprise that greeted such a direct answer from such an unlikely source.

"I couldn't ever find anyone guilty," she said.

Mr. Hislop frowned, but decided to let the matter rest there for the moment.

Not so Gwen who leaned across the table and said, "There isn't a death penalty any longer if that's what is worrying you."

Joyce Stanley nodded. "Yes, I know that," she said, as she retired once more behind her smile which seemed suddenly to have taken on an enigmatic quality.

It was only after the trial had started she had realised that whatever her feelings about the accused and his conduct, it didn't lie in her to convict a fellow creature of murder, despite twelve of her peers having done precisely that to her. It wasn't perverseness so much as an unforeseen aversion to a system which was capable of such vagaries in its operation.

"Mr. Upham?"

"I reckon he's guilty."

"Ms. Hackford?"

"I've no doubt about his guilt."

"Mr. Floyd?"

"I'm for guilty," the juror said, as if setting a bold example.

"Mr. Capper?"

"I think he did it, but that the prosecution hasn't produced enough evidence."

"Then you're saying not guilty," Mr. Hislop observed coldly.

"If you ask me," Martin added, "it's what the judge thinks too. You could tell from the way she summed up."

A number of jurors looked at him with respect and Martin sat back with a complacent air.

"What about you?" Floyd asked, fixing the foreman with a sharp look.

"My view is that we need to have a good deal more discussion."

At one o'clock there was a knock on the door and the jury bailiff, who had been sitting on a chair in the corridor outside (except when putting his ear to the keyhole), handed in plates of sandwiches and jugs of tea and coffee. This he did without uttering a word and to the point of ignoring one of Peter Floyd's sallies.

"He's not allowed to speak to us without the judge's approval," Gwen explained. "We might otherwise be influenced by something he said."

"I once met somebody who'd sat on a jury and he said how the bailiff had helped them by mentioning the accused's previous convictions," Floyd remarked.

"All I can say is that it was highly improper of him to do so," Gwen retorted.

Discussion continued while they ate and afterwards.

Mrs. Norrington couldn't think why the accused

hadn't notified the police, but seemed unwilling to draw any fatal inferences from his failure.

Reg Upham, who had customers living in Little Misten, said that Mrs. Wimble had been very well liked locally, but not her husband. This brought forth a rebuke from the foreman who said they must only concern themselves with evidence given in court.

Gwen kept on saying it was so obvious what had happened, she couldn't understand why anyone had difficulty drawing the same inference as herself.

Peter Floyd exhorted them to look at the case as a whole and not get bogged down in pernickety detail. This produced various protesting murmurs.

Martin said he couldn't understand why only the deceased's hand had come to light, and this was the cause of one of his major doubts.

Mr. Hislop's efforts to control the discussion were only intermittently successful, as people darted from one topic to another with the tireless energy of a dog trying to pick up an uncertain scent.

At one stage, Gwen and Peter Floyd exchanged acrimonious views about the weight that should be given to Maureen Yates's evidence. It took Reg Upham to point out that they'd both voted the same way in the preliminary round.

Mrs. Norrington was bothered that they'd not been told what had happened to the deceased's sleeping pills and was reminded that over two months had elapsed between Mrs. Wimble's disappearance and first entry on the scene by the police in the shape of P.C. Jameson.

Joyce Stanley, meanwhile, merely kept on smiling, giving an occasional nod when something further was required.

At three o'clock another vote was taken which resulted in three for guilty, six for not guilty and three still not sure.

By three thirty, the three unsures had joined up with the not guilties.

Peter Floyd, who had unbuttoned his shirt collar and loosened his tie, now said tetchily, "If it's going to help, I'll switch sides. That seems to be what the majority want and I'm prepared to go along with their view if it'll get us out of this bloody room."

"You may be prepared to compromise your principles, but I'm not," Gwen said contemptuously.

"Who's talking about principles?" Floyd asked. "It's a question of facing reality. We're obviously not going to persuade the majority to find him guilty, so we might as well gracefully acknowledge the fact. Or ungracefully if you prefer."

Half an hour later, Gwen Hackford found herself in a minority of one after Reg Upham had said he reckoned they'd all had enough.

"Why are you so certain he's guilty?" he asked Gwen.

"It's the only explanation of her disappearance that fits the facts."

"I still think he's probably guilty," Reg said mildly, "but I've persuaded myself there's a reasonable doubt."

"My head's going round so much that I don't know a reasonable doubt from an unreasonable one," Mrs. Norrington murmured sadly.

"All doubts have to be resolved in favor of the accused," Mr. Hislop said mechanically, as though somebody had inserted a coin into him to obtain this contribution.

"Look, Gwen," Floyd said suddenly, "would you be prepared to find him guilty if you knew he'd be hanged?"

"That's not a fair question," she said, after a slight hesitation. "You're introducing an emotive element."

"But would you?"

"I refuse to answer such a hypothetical question," she said loftily.

"Is there anything we've not touched on that might help?" Mr. Hislop asked in a weary voice.

"We've not only touched on everything," Peter Floyd replied, "we've ridden round the course at least half a dozen times." He gazed helplessly at his fellow jurors. "Can't we give a majority verdict of eleven to one? Who knows how it works?"

"The judge would have to give us a further direction," Gwen said, unable to resist showing off her legal knowledge.

"As long as ten of us agree, it's all right," Martin added. "I remember a lawyer giving us a lecture at school and saying that majority verdicts were a recent innovation."

"So you can't win anyway, Gwen," Floyd said. "Why not give in now and save us this further rigmarole with the judge?"

"It's a matter of principle," she said, but with less conviction than hitherto. Then suddenly she burst out, "Oh, all right, if he's going to be acquitted anyway, be it on all your heads."

A corporate sigh of relief went up, as Peter Floyd leapt to the door, before any change of heart could take place, to tell the bailiff they were ready to return a verdict. Even Mr. Hislop didn't protest at having the matter taken out of his hands.

After all the nerve-shredding hours of wrangling, what followed was brief to the point of anti-climax.

Mrs. Justice Gentry received the verdict without any sign of surprise or disapproval. She immediately discharged Frank Wimble who turned toward the jury and gave them a small, impassive bow.

Maureen Yates broke down and sobbed with relief when the news was conveyed to her outside the court-room by Graham Tapling. She had not felt able to face the strain of waiting inside.

A few minutes later she and Wimble were re-united and hugged and kissed each other, surrounded by well-wishers and reporters.

As the jurors walked by on their way to claim their expenses, Frank Wimble tried to catch the eye of several of them. Most, however, looked determinedly the other way.

Only Peter Floyd glanced across, gave him a wink and called out "good luck." He regarded himself as the only realist amongst them. After all, who could afford to pass up the possibility of future business with a millionaire? Even one who had probably murdered his wife.

Part 4

1

Frank Wimble and Maureen were smuggled out of the court-house by a side entrance under cover of darkness, whence they drove up to London to spend the night at Maureen's sister's flat, where they reckoned to be safe from the press.

Maureen was so happy herself over the result of the trial that she failed to notice Frank's more subdued mood. Or rather, she noticed, but misinterpreted it. She believed it to be a natural reaction after all the months of strain and was sure she would quickly be able to entice him out of it. Her sole thought now was how soon she could become Mrs. Frank Wimble, with all that that implied.

When they reached the flat, they drank a bottle of champagne which had been left on ice for them. Then they went to bed and made love. Later they got up, drank more champagne and had a light meal while they watched a late T.V. show. After which it was time to go to bed again.

He dropped off to sleep almost at once, but woke up two or three hours later when everything around was still and silent.

After a while, he got out of bed and went into the living-room where he lit a cigarette and moved over to the window. He pulled back the curtains and stared out at the deserted street.

Ever since he had stepped from the dock a free man, he had known he would have to return to the scene of his crime if he was to have any peace of mind. It was vital to satisfy himself that no other parts of Elspeth's body could possibly come to light. If necessary, he must be prepared to rebury her remains. As only bones would be left, he could remove these in a sack and throw them into a deep pond miles from anywhere.

The discovery of her hand had, apart from anything else, been a humiliation to someone who had never doubted his ability to commit the perfect murder. He now realised what had gone wrong. He hadn't buried her deep enough, though this wasn't entirely his fault. The fact was that the dry summer had left the ground uncommonly hard. Far more so than he had expected to find it. In the event he had had to content himself with covering her body with a light sprinkling of earth and with an abundance of leaf mould and bracken. It had looked perfect by the light of his torch, but it had obviously not been sufficient to deter some creature with burrowing instincts.

He would think of an excuse for not coming home the next evening and would drive down to make sure once and for all that he couldn't be subjected to any further disagreeable surprises.

With this settled in his mind, he returned to bed and quickly fell into a dreamless sleep.

When he awoke the next morning, he could smell coffee and could hear Maureen moving about in the kitchen.

"Hello, darling, so you've woken up," she said, coming into the room and bending over the bed to give him a kiss. "I was about to bring you breakfast in bed."

"I'd sooner get up," he said, throwing back the covers. "You ought to have woken me earlier."

"But why, darling? You need all the sleep and rest you can get for the next few days. We can have a lovely day of doing nothing."

He shook his head. "I must start picking up the threads of my various interests. God knows what I'll discover. You may even find yourself married to a pauper. And you wouldn't like that, would you?"

"Don't be so silly, darling! You know everything's been well looked after while you've been out of action."

"I've still got to get back and find out for myself. There'll be decisions that have been hanging fire..." He paused in the act of scratching his stomach. "Give me three days to deal with the immediate problems and then I'll take you away for a long weekend. Where'd you like to go? Paris? Monte Carlo? You say and I'll make the arrangements today."

"Mmm, I think Paris. You can't be certain of the weather on the Mediterranean at this time of year."

"O.K., Paris it'll be. We'll fly over on Friday and stay till Tuesday."

"When are you planning to throw your party?" she asked, following him into the bathroom.

"*Our* party. I've decided to make it a New Year's Eve party at Downview Lodge."

"You don't want to spend Christmas there, do you?" she said with a slight frown.

"We'll spend it wherever you like. Here in London. Or we can go back to Paris."

"I don't think I'll ever enjoy staying at Downview Lodge again. Not after all that's happened."

"I'll probably sell it later on, but first I'm going to hold the party there. I want to show the local people that I've not run away. I'm looking forward to making quite a few of them choke with embarrassment on my gracious hospitality."

"Who else are you going to ask?"

"I thought I might invite Alan Coe. I'd like to have the judge there just to show I don't harbour any ill-feelings but I don't expect she'd come. I'll see what Graham Tapling thinks. And I must find out the name of that juror who wished me good luck. I promise you it'll be a bloody good party. I'll have caterers down from London and it'll be a no-expense-spared affair." Observing her slightly apprehensive expression in the bathroom mirror, "You can ask anyone you like as well."

"You really mean to prove something, don't you?" she said.

"That I don't run away because of a bit of trouble," he replied with a small grim nod.

There was a silence while she watched him shaving, handling the razor with brisk, competent motions.

As he finished, she said, "There is one thing we've not yet talked about, Frank. How soon can we get married?"

"Soon," he said after a slight pause. "Tell you what, we'll make it a joint New Year's Eve and engagement party. We'll announce our forthcoming marriage to the world."

"Can't we get married before then?" she said, in a faintly querulous voice.

"I must have a bit of time to get my life back on course," he remarked. "We'll discuss a date when we're in Paris. After all, we're only going to run round the corner to the register office. We're not hiring Westminster Abbey for the occasion."

"But I've waited so long to become your wife," she said, with a sigh.

"I know. And very soon you will be. We'll get married immediately after the party."

"Why can't we before?"

"Let's get Christmas and the New Year out of the way first. What about this for an idea? We'll fix a date early in January and go straight off to the Caribbean for a couple of weeks afterwards. How does that strike you? Or we can make it the Seychelles if you prefer," he added in a placatory tone.

He knew that she had been expecting they would be married within days of his acquittal, but he wasn't prepared to be rushed. He wanted to marry her and intended to marry her, so why couldn't she let it rest there? If it came to it, she didn't have any choice.

Shortly after half past nine, he stepped out into the street and did something he'd not done for nearly a year. Hailed a cab.

Toward the end of the morning, he called Maureen to tell her he had made all the arrangements for their weekend in Paris. As an apparent afterthought, he added that he was already immersed in meetings and wouldn't be able to get home until late.

"How late, darling?" she asked.

"Very late. So mind you warm up the bed."

2

.

One of his worst bits of luck, he reckoned, was being observed by Dr. Farrer. Normally, not more than two or three cars a night used the road past Downview Lodge. Fortunately, he had been able to provide an explanation which the jury had obviously swallowed. At any rate, they had not choked on it.

Apart from the fact that FW 01 was still in the garage at Downview Lodge, he had no intention of being caught that way again.

On this occasion, he hired a car of popular make which had a wholly unmemorable registration number. Five miles out of Little Misten he turned off the main road and approached his goal by a series of lanes. Not until he was absolutely certain there were no cars either behind or in front of him did he manoeuvre his way along a track which dipped almost at once into a heavily wooded valley.

He switched off his lights as soon as he made the turn, feeling his way by the hedges on either side which were outlined against the night sky.

It was just after eleven o'clock.

Fifty yards inside the wood, he reached a point

where the track forked and where he had left the car on the previous occasion. He stopped and switched off the engine.

Elspeth's grave was some thirty yards from where he now stood, about ten yards from the track on its left side. He recalled how he had first tried to dig it on the opposite side, but had found the ground too hard. He had then moved across to the other side where the bracken was thicker and the earth fractionally less unyielding to his spade.

Elspeth's body had lain wrapped in a blanket beside him as he dug. It had been a clever idea to render her unconscious with a massive overdose of her own sleeping tablets and even if she wasn't actually dead when he buried her, she couldn't have known anything of what was happening.

He recalled the grim urgency with which he had set about his task and how he had been almost deafened by the thumping of his own heart, the exertion and a sudden fear that had gripped him sending his blood pounding through his body.

He realised as he now began to walk purposefully along the left-hand fork how different everything looked. The trees were bare and he could see the sky through a web of tangled branches. On the last occasion, the leaves were only starting to fall and the sky had been invisible.

Nevertheless, he was sure he would recognise the spot at which he had left the track and plunged into the brushwood. All too soon, however, came the realisation that he must have passed it. He retraced his steps, only to find himself back at the car.

Clearly his recollection was at fault and he had not penetrated far enough. Why the hell did it have to look so different?

Once more he hurried along the track, pausing at

intervals to try and get his bearings. On this occasion he reached a small clearing where timber lay stacked awaiting collection.

Oh, God, he thought, that's why he'd not recognised the spot. They'd been cutting down the bloody trees. Half walking, half running he returned along the track to a point which had to be near enough where he had plunged into the undergrowth and dug.

He cursed himself for not having a clearer recollection of the ground's configuration. If only he had memorised the position of at least one or two individual trees. But never having been a countryman, one tree was to him the same as another.

He thrust his way through undergrowth and, with the aid of his flashlight, examined an area where Elspeth might lie buried.

During the next forty minutes he made a number of spot checks without finding a single trace of where he had dug her grave.

He returned grimly to the car and got in. For two or three minutes, he sat trying to assemble his thoughts.

Even if there had been some tree-felling, Elspeth's remains couldn't have been disturbed, or he'd have heard. That meant her body must still lie safely buried even though he had been unable to locate the spot. And with each week that passed, the chance of any further remains being discovered must surely diminish.

Another reassuring thought came to him. You couldn't be tried a second time for the same offence, so his acquittal had put an end to that possibility.

Admittedly, it would have been more satisfactory to have been able to make positively certain that everything was all right, but that was not to be. He picked up the sack which he had so carefully brought with him and shoved it beneath his seat. He hadn't relished the prospect of transporting Elspeth's bones to another burial place and was now, at least, spared that.

He reached London without any untoward incident and let himself into the flat. Before going to the bedroom, he had a large brandy, which he felt he had more than earned.

Maureen was fast asleep, which was probably just as well.

3

About a week before Christmas Isabelle Gentry was invited out to dinner by her brother-in-law, Tom. He always entertained her in the ladies' annexe of his club in St. James's, which had the advantage of being quiet and comfortable and of serving surprisingly good food.

"How long have you been back in London?" he asked, after he had ordered drinks.

"Only three days."

"Are you out on circuit again in the new year?"

She shook her head. "I'll be in London all next term, including a stint at the Old Bailey."

Their drinks arrived and he lifted his glass to toast his guest. "It's always a delight seeing you, Isabelle. Incidentally, the last time we met Peter was having a bit of trouble with his marriage. What's the latest score there?"

Isabelle rested her glass of dry sherry on the table at her side. "His wife returned to him after a few days and they're still together. All one can do is cross one's fingers. The most hopeful thing is that the widower neighbour, who was the cause of the trouble, is selling up and moving to South Africa."

"He can't go much further than that," Tom observed drily.

"It should help Fran to settle down when she's no longer in danger of running into him round every corner."

"Are you spending Christmas with them?"

"No, I'm going to John and his family on Christmas day and having both boys, their wives and five grandchildren to lunch at my flat the day after."

"Great heavens, how do you fit them all in?"

"It'll be chaos, but I'll love it. It's not often we manage a complete family get-together. One problem is that my two daughters-in-law don't particularly like each other, but it's all right provided they don't see one another too often."

The head waiter brought them menus and took their order. "I'll let you know when your table's ready, sir," he said, as he departed.

"Let's have another drink," Tom said. "There's no hurry to eat." It was while they were having their second drink he remarked, "I see that fellow you were trying at Dinsford got off. Was that the right result?"

"I'd have you know I usually get the right results in my cases," she said with a smile.

"I'm sure you do. I didn't intend to cast a slur on your judicial talent."

Isabelle gave a laugh. "Of course you didn't. Yes, I think it was the right result on the evidence."

"You mean, he did it but there wasn't enough proof?"

"If he didn't do it, I can't account for his behaving so equivocally afterwards. He obviously had something to hide."

"I remember your saying when I called at the lodgings that lunchtime that the case had a number of puzzling features."

She nodded. "One more puzzling than all the rest. Namely, why has only her hand ever come to light?"

"Perhaps he dismembered her body and buried the parts over a wide area."

"There was evidence that he was apt to faint at the sight of blood and I can't see him having cut her body up in those circumstances."

"He may have chopped off her hands so that she couldn't be identified by fingerprints."

"Possible, but not at all likely."

"Incidentally, I'm surprised he didn't remove her wedding ring."

"Quite possibly it wouldn't come off. Mine won't since I've had rheumatism in that joint, not that there was any evidence of such in her case."

"I imagine juries are happier when they have definite evidence as to cause of death."

"Certainly. So am I. On the other hand, murder cases without bodies ever being found have multiplied in recent times."

The head waiter appeared to tell them their table was ready when they were, and they got up to go into the dining-room.

After they had sat down, she said with a wry smile, "Edward, my clerk, was telling me this morning that Frank Wimble is giving a great New Year's Eve party at Downview Lodge and is asking all the locals to come and meet the next Mrs. Wimble."

"How thick-skinned can you be!"

"Edward read it in the gossip column of one of the papers which also reported Wimble as saying he'd thought of inviting me to his party."

"The brazenness of the fellow!"

"You can't keep a good millionaire down," she re-marked.

"I wonder what is the explanation of only her hand being found," he said, thoughtfully.

"I'd dearly like to know. Nobody has yet come up with anything approaching a plausible answer. It was that failure more than anything else that made me sum up as I did."

4

The outside caterers arrived at Downview Lodge soon after nine o'clock on the morning of 31st December. The advance party parked their magenta-coloured van in the drive next to the postman's bright red one, thereby presenting a vision for the colour-blind only.

Although there were only four of them (a girl and three men), they seemed to take over the whole ground floor within seconds of their entry. Frank Wimble decided to leave Maureen to deal with them.

Glancing at the mail the postman had handed to him at the door, he retired into the small front room, which was the warmest in the house. Shortly after his acquittal Mrs. Passingham had left a note saying that she wouldn't be coming any more and he had since heard that her husband had died. The upshot was that nobody had been looking after the house on a regular basis during the greater part of December.

He and Maureen had spent Christmas in London at one of the large hotels and had only come down to Little Misten the previous evening. He reckoned it was going to take all the caterers' energy and ingenuity to give the place a festive air by nightfall. They were charging enough for their services, however, and had confidently predicted he would be a fully satisfied customer.

Closing the door behind him, he examined the mail more closely. Two of the envelopes clearly contained end-of-year bills. There were four charitable appeals which he dropped unread into the waste-paper basket.

In fact, only one letter had any look of interest. It bore a first class stamp and had been posted in central London the previous day. It was a typewritten envelope without any indication of the sender.

Slitting it open with his thumb-nail, he peered inside with mild curiosity. There were two folded sheets of paper, giving off an unmistakable perfume. As he recognised the writing his heart seemed to stop.

Elspeth's hand had always been distinctive and neat, and on the small side for a woman.

He walked over to a chair and sat down before bringing himself to read it.

The door suddenly flew open and Maureen burst in, halting abruptly in her tracks with a look of alarm.

"What on earth's happened, Frank?" she cried out.

He shook his head impatiently.

"Nothing," he murmured.

"But you look terrible, darling. Are you all right? Shall I send for a doctor? For God's sake tell me what's wrong."

"I'm all right."

"Don't be silly, darling, you're anything but all right." Her eye alighted on the letter half-concealed in his hand. "Have you had some bad news?"

"Just leave me alone and I'll be all right in a moment."

"It's something in that letter you're holding, isn't it?" she went on in an anxious voice. "What's happened, darling?"

"I'll tell you later. Now be a good girl and leave me. I want to sit and think a few minutes."

She left the room with a show of extreme reluctance and he walked over and locked the door behind her.

Then, returning to his chair, he unfolded the letter and began to read it, mesmerised by its contents.

Dear Frank, (he read)
This should reach you on the day of your party, when I gather you are proposing to present the future Mrs. Wimble to your guests. I'm afraid, therefore, it will come as a nasty shock to you to learn that the past Mrs. Wimble (as you believed her to be) is still very much alive. Although I no longer live in England, I followed your trial with interest. But now, it seems to me, the time has arrived to declare myself and send you my terms.

In the first place, you can't, of course, marry Maureen without committing bigamy which, I don't suppose, will please her very much. It will also inevitably put a damper on your celebration party, but you'll hardly expect me to be sympathetic about that.

Since you didn't murder me, I suppose it's fair that you got off, though it wasn't for any lack of trying on your part. You were certainly guilty of an attempt to kill me when you tried to get me to take that overdose of sleeping tablets. Fortunately they have a bitter taste when dissolved and I was alerted and able to pour the concoction away while you were out of the room. I was also distinctly suspicious on account of your suddenly being so thoughtful and solicitous that evening. That made me more nervous than anything. As soon as I took a sip of the drink you handed me, I realised you had doctored it and, presumably, for one purpose only. It seemed best to pretend it had had its effect, as, otherwise, you might have decided to kill me immediately by some other means. When you wrapped me in a blanket and carried me out to the car, I knew at once what you had in mind. When we arrived at that wood, I was ready, if necessary, to jump up and make a dash for it, even at the risk of being chased and felled. You'd certainly have overcome any squeamishness in those extreme circumstances, wouldn't you, Frank? However, when it became apparent you were only able to dig a shallow grave, I thought it best to act my role of corpse to the bitter end. As soon as you had driven off, however, I rose from the dead.

I'm glad to think you had several months of hell after your arrest. It's no more than you deserved. At the beginning you were really getting away far too easily with what you'd done, so it seemed only just that the police should find some evidence of the crime you believed you had committed.

I take it you will continue to live with Maureen even if you can't now marry her; though whether she'll be happy with such an arrangement is another matter. In any event, that's your problem and not mine.

For myself, I have no intention of ever turning up in your life again, though I require a substantial financial settlement. An outright payment of £500,000 is a small price for you to pay in the circumstances. It will ensure my silence, which, I admit, is also in my own interest. That, at least, gives you a guarantee of sorts.

I should love to see your face as you read this and

even more so when you greet your guests this evening.
If you happen to notice a fly on the wall, you'd better
swat it while you can, for it'll almost certainly be me!
I'll send you details of how I want the money remitted
within the next few days. Probably a draft to a num-
bered bank account in Zurich will be best. Inciden-
tally, I'm not living in Switzerland, but a bank
account there is most useful.

Your still living wife, Elspeth.

P.S. I've not dated this letter, but it is being written on
Christmas Eve with the intention that you shall re-
ceive it in exactly a week's time.

When guests began arriving around nine thirty that
evening, they found the drive hung with coloured
lights and the front of the house floodlit. A wave of
bright warmth enveloped them as they stepped inside to be welcomed by Graham Tapling and his be-
mused-looking wife.

The solicitor explained that their host and his fi-
ancee had been struck down in mid-afternoon by a
sudden severe attack of food poisoning, which was
attributed to some tinned oysters they had eaten.

After appropriate medication, they had driven
back to their flat in London to rest, but had left the
firmest instructions that the party must go ahead.
They sent everyone their apologies and best wishes
for an enjoyable evening.

Though he knew that food poisoning was only an
excuse, Tapling was unaware of the exact nature of
what had happened. All Frank Wimble would tell
him was that he had received some shattering news
which made it impossible for him to play host that
evening.

The solicitor had tried to find out more from

Maureen, only to discover that she, too, was in the dark as to what had happened.

The free-loaders, who comprised at least half the guests, were not particularly bothered by the absence of their host. Provided the drink didn't run out, they weren't going to worry.

Those guests who had come chiefly out of curiosity were to depart again without it being satisfied.

Peter Floyd, who had received an invitation with a mixture of pleasure and high expectation, reflecting that his good wishes to Wimble after his acquittal had paid their first dividend, was disappointed to be greeted by a stand-in host, who gave him a quick, embarrassed handshake.

Meanwhile, as their guests made merry at Downview Lodge, Frank and Maureen sat with a rapidly emptying bottle of brandy between them.

Maureen had been crying and her face had a pinched, anxious look. His expression was morose.

He had refused to let her read Elspeth's letter, but had told her from whom the letter had come.

He had known he would have to tell her something and would in any event soon have to explain why they could no longer get married on the date that had been fixed in the following week.

In the circumstances, he decided to concoct a story that would reflect least damagingly on himself. Accordingly, he described how on that fateful Friday evening, Elspeth had suddenly attacked him with a knife; how he had managed to disarm her, but how she had then come at him with her hands. In the struggle that followed, she had suddenly slumped to the floor, apparently dead. He had certainly not strangled her, but he knew how some people, particularly when in an emotional state, have an especially sensitive vagus nerve in their necks, the merest con-

243

tact with which can cause them to die of vagal inhibition. This was what appeared to have happened to Elspeth. Realising, however, that his story would never be believed in view of the recent history of their marriage, he had decided to bury her body, believing her to be dead, when in fact she could only have been in some sort of coma...

"Why on earth didn't you tell me all this sooner?" Maureen asked in an anguished tone.

"Would you have believed me?" he said, with a small boy's ruefulness.

"Of course I would. But what are we going to do, Frank? It's wicked what she's done to you, she ought to go to prison for it. She's a really evil woman. I don't know why you didn't immediately tell Graham so that he can do something. She mustn't be allowed to get away with it."

His only response was to pour himself another brandy. He had more or less decided to give his solicitor the same bowdlerised version he had given Maureen. Not that Tapling, of course, would believe him. But who cared? He didn't employ him to accept every word he uttered, but rather to give him sound legal advice and get him out of jams without asking too many awkward questions.

Even without any lawyer's advice, he reckoned that Elspeth was certainly guilty of something. In the first place, however, she was out of England and, secondly, he suspected that her own crime would probably be regarded as less heinous than his. And, most important of all, he failed to see how he could use the law to wreak his revenge on her without further harm to himself.

That was the real crux of the situation. Moreover, it was clearly how she, too, saw it. In brief, she had him by the short and curlies and both of them knew it.

With a hand that shook, he reached out for the brandy bottle.

"Some New Year's Eve," he remarked sourly, as he tossed back another half-glassful, while Maureen sat with eyes shut and head throbbing. "And to think of all those bloody people boozing away at my expense. The best part of four thousand pounds down the drain." His voice, heavily slurred, trailed away as he added, "And that's only a beginning..."

5

"It's time we left for the airport, Brian," Elspeth Wimble called out to her son. "She'll panic if we're not there when the plane gets in."

"Nothing could make *her* panic."

Elspeth laughed. "You're probably right, but my new year's resolution is to be punctual and I don't want to break it on the very first day of the year." She gave her son an affectionate look as he came into the room. "I keep on wondering how the party went last night..."

"Provided your letter arrived in time, I would assume the answer to be, disastrously. Though, to give father his due, he's capable of brazening out most things."

"I hope it did reach him yesterday."

"I posted it mid-morning at the Trafalgar Square post office just before I left for Heathrow, so it had no excuse not to arrive the next day."

"I wish you didn't have to go back to England," she said in a worried voice, after a brief pause.

"Nothing'll happen. Father's certainly not going to take your letter to the police and, even if he did, there's absolutely no evidence that I had any part in his undoing."

"Can't they say you fabricated evidence by planting that hand with my ring on its finger?"

"It may be what father deduces, but there's absolutely no proof. The hospital has no record of one of its bodies being taken away for burial short of a hand. The unfortunate woman was so mangled in a car crash that she was brought in more or less in pieces."

Elspeth gave a shiver. "God rest her soul!" she murmured.

"That's more than father ever said for yours when he thought you were dead," Brian said implacably. "Anyway, I'm hoping to emigrate to Canada. I already have the forms."

"Have you been in touch with Alison since the trial?" his mother asked, after another silence.

"We exchanged Christmas cards. She wrote on hers that she and William would not be going to the party and that she didn't suppose I'd been invited."

"When the dust has settled, I'd like to get in touch with her. Even if we never did see eye to eye, she's still my daughter."

"Her husband's a right little prig," Brian remarked, acerbically. "Come on, mum, it really is time we left."

It was an hour's drive to the airport under the warm Spanish sun. As they parked the car and got out, they could see the plane with its British markings taxiing to the terminal.

Brian noticed his mother blink away tears as they positioned themselves at the gate where arriving passengers emerged from customs and immigration checks.

"I hope she caught the plane all right," Elspeth

said anxiously, as she scanned the faces of the first arrivals. "I doubt whether I'd have survived if it hadn't been for her. She saved my life in more senses than one and I'll never forget those two days she looked after me..."

Brian gave his mother's arm a comforting squeeze.

"Now, don't get all worked up, mum," he said in a firm voice.

"Look, Brian," Elspeth suddenly burst out, "there she is."

Ada Passingham stood staring about her with the same forbidding expression she had worn in the witness box at Dinsford Crown Court. She had a headscarf knotted beneath her chin and was wearing a thick tweed coat buttoned to the neck.

"Just look at her," Elspeth said in a choked voice. "Isn't she splendid? Not a concession to the Spanish sun—or to anyone."

Mrs. Passingham suddenly caught sight of them and her upper lip began visibly to tremble as she came with arms outstretched toward Elspeth.

For the first time in their lives the two women hugged one another while Brian looked on with a dispassionate air.

The last twelve months had been utterly nerve-racking for them all and he hoped that the year which lay ahead would prove itself as uneventful as a party political broadcast.

He had no regrets about what he had done. His father's conduct after his wife's so-called disappearance had been a monstrous affront which demanded punitive action. It had become absolutely necessary to teach him a lesson.

Whether or not he had learnt the right one remained to be seen.